"There's Only One Kind of Help
You Can Give Me, Lane."

"I don't see how I can give you *any* help," she said stiffly. "As far as I can tell, we aren't working on the same project, nor are we aiming for the same goals."

He raised one eyebrow. "Aren't we?" he teased, his eyes glinting intimately. "Don't we have at least one of the same goals?"

She felt heat rush into her cheeks at his insinuation. "No, we don't, Vance. We have nothing at all in common."

"Then I must have misunderstood," he replied calmly. "We need to . . . talk . . . about this."

GENA DALTON
is a wife and mother as well as a writer, but her interests don't stop there. She is fascinated by Ozark-Appalachian folk culture, does tole painting, gardens, and is interested in horses.

Dear Reader,

Silhouette Special Editions are an exciting new line of contemporary romances from Silhouette Books. Special Editions are written specifically for our readers who want a story with heightened romantic tension.

Special Editions have all the elements you've enjoyed in Silhouette Romances and *more*. These stories concentrate on romance in a longer, more realistic and sophisticated way, and they feature greater sensual detail.

I hope you enjoy this book and all the wonderful romances from Silhouette.

Karen Solem
Editor-in-Chief
Silhouette Books

GENA DALTON
April Encounter

Silhouette Special Edition
Published by Silhouette Books New York
America's Publisher of Contemporary Romance

Silhouette Books by Gena Dalton

Sorrel Sunset (SE #69)
April Encounter (SE #142)

SILHOUETTE BOOKS, a Division of Simon & Schuster, Inc.
1230 Avenue of the Americas, New York, N.Y. 10020

Copyright © 1984 by Gena Dalton

Distributed by Pocket Books

All rights reserved, including the right to reproduce
this book or portions thereof in any form whatsoever.
For information address Silhouette Books, 1230 Avenue
of the Americas, New York, N.Y. 10020

ISBN: 0-671-53647-8

First Silhouette Books printing February, 1984

10 9 8 7 6 5 4 3 2 1

All of the characters in this book are fictitious. Any resem-
blance to actual persons, living or dead, is purely coincidental.

Map by Ray Lundgren

SILHOUETTE, SILHOUETTE SPECIAL EDITION and
colophon are registered trademarks of Simon & Schuster, Inc.

America's Publisher of Contemporary Romance

Printed in the U.S.A.

For my sisters,
with love and appreciation

April Encounter

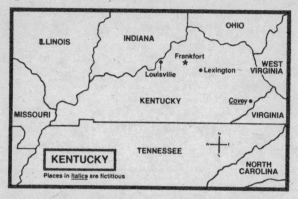

ILLINOIS

INDIANA

OHIO

Frankfort
★
Louisville
• Lexington

WEST
VIRGINIA

MISSOURI

KENTUCKY

Covey •

VIRGINIA

TENNESSEE

NORTH
CAROLINA

N
W E
S

KENTUCKY

Places in _italics_ are fictitious

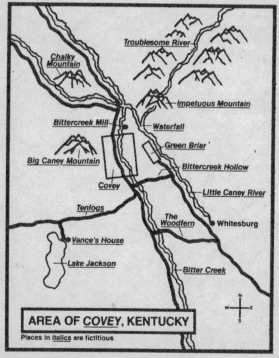

Troublesome River

_Chalky
Mountain_

Impetuous Mountain

Bittercreek Mill

Waterfall

Green Briar

Big Caney Mountain

Bittercreek Hollow

Little Caney River

Covey

Tenlogs

_The
Woodfern_

• Whitesburg

• _Vance's House_

Lake Jackson

Bitter Creek

N
W E
S

AREA OF _COVEY_, KENTUCKY

Places in _italics_ are fictitious

Chapter One

Lane stepped out into the early morning mistiness and stood very still, savoring the solitude and the feeling of being close to the earth that the mountains always gave her. She drew a deep breath of the heavy air, filled with the scents of pines and April blossoms. The Cumberlands towered close on every side, enclosing her in a pale green world traced with shades of brown.

She crossed the wooden footbridge and began following the path that wound between the narrow, paved road and the rocky creek that ran in front of her new dwelling, Alice MacDonald's two-story clapboard home. She hoped she could remember the directions Alice had given her; a roaring waterfall would be perfect for a morning like this.

Soon she left the edge of the small town of Covey, Kentucky, and when the path divided after a quarter of a mile she took the right-hand fork and began to climb. Four summers of studying folkways in the mountains had taught her what to wear, and in her laced hiking boots she moved easily over the rough ground strewn with rocks, tree limbs and deep pockets of dead leaves.

Mixed with the browns of the leaves, the pale light showed delicate yellow violets and tiny pink hepaticas, their leaves a darker green than the nearby ferns and patches of new grass. Lane had an impulse to stop and just enjoy them, but she wanted to see the waterfall at sunrise and the light was steadily becoming stronger.

At last she climbed over the highest ridge and emerged from the forest onto the top of a boulder that dropped steeply into the valley on the other side. For a moment she couldn't spot the fall, but she could hear its roar in the distance. Her eyes adjusted to the stronger light, and she searched the rocks and trees on the wall across the chasm. Then she saw it: torrents of water tumbling wildly from a height many feet above her head. The sky was pink and yellow all along the horizon above it and the water fell from shadow into light. She couldn't take her eyes away. The sight combined with the sound of it held her mesmerized.

"Magnificent, isn't it?" a deep voice asked.

Her heart raced suddenly with the realization that she wasn't alone. She turned. A tall man was at the edge of the trees, one foot propped on a large rock, his arm resting casually across his knee. Her startled gaze met dark brown, almost black, eyes that were alert and cynical and interested all at the same time.

"I . . . I didn't see you," Lane stammered finally. She was reassured by his respectable appearance, but the compelling magnetism of his gaze was almost as unsettling as her initial fear had been.

He nodded. "You couldn't see anything but the falls," he agreed, smiling slightly. "You must be a real nature lover."

She smiled back, her heart thudding against her ribs. "I suppose I am." Not only was her heart still beating rapidly, but her hands were trembling. It was cool, but not that cold, she thought, as she shoved her hands into the pockets of her quilted vest. Was he doing this to her?

He was still leaning on the rock, looking at her with that confident, almost bemused expression on his handsome, square face.

"What about you?" she ventured. "What are you doing way up here at this time of the morning?"

"Oh . . ." He hesitated. "I just wanted to see how things look from here."

His eyes left hers and swept the mountain facing them and the river valley between the two rocky walls. Her gaze followed his as he looked into the distance downstream and several yellow specks across the shallow river caught her attention.

"Are those bulldozers?" she asked incredulously.

He answered with a matter-of-fact, very sure, "Yes."

"I can't believe it!" she exclaimed, surprise and dismay coloring her voice and causing a sinking feeling in her stomach. "Surely people aren't going to come all the way in here and start tearing up the valleys and moving the mountains around! What could they possibly be building this far back in the hills?"

He looked back at her quickly, his glance sharp. "This isn't exactly the end of the earth. After all, we're not too far from the interstate highway—or from the state park or the national forest."

"Oh, I suppose that's true," Lane replied, impatiently brushing back a wisp of her hair that had come loose from her braids onto her forehead. "It's just that I like to think of some places as being far enough away from civilization to stay unspoiled." She sighed. "What in the world are they doing there, anyway?" she asked, leaning forward to get a better view of the machines.

"It's going to be an amusement park."

She stared at him, astonished, her blue eyes wide and still in her heart-shaped face.

"Oh, no," she said, her words almost a moan. "It'll change everything for miles around." Her gaze moved lovingly to the forest, the valley, the waterfall, again. "None of this will ever, ever be the same."

He shrugged. "There's always someone who says that about any kind of progress," he replied.

"But it's true!" she insisted. "How can you stand here in the middle of all this . . . this . . ." She looked around again, words failing her. Her eyes fell on a patch of the early yellow violets growing in a nest of fallen limbs.

She moved quickly to the flowers, dropping to her knees and motioning to him. "Look at these, just look," she ordered, cupping several of them in her hand. The damp, woodsy smell of the forest floor rose into the foggy air. "How can it be progress to wipe these out?" she demanded.

"How can it not be progress to give jobs to

hundreds of people?" he countered. He had moved to follow her, and now he was looming above her on long legs, his thigh muscles hard and taut under tight corduroy jeans. His feet were planted wide apart, and his arms were crossed belligerently on his chest.

She tilted her head to one side and stared up into his impassive face. A confidence that bordered on arrogance emanated from him; everything about him shouted that he was accustomed to being right, to being the one in command.

Her blue eyes flashed, and now it was anger that made her hands shake. "There's always someone who says that about any kind of so-called progress," she said sarcastically, throwing his own words back at him. "You can't justify ruining the land simply by saying that people will have jobs." She felt her cheeks flush and her pulse beat harder as the bitter words burst from her.

For an endless moment he stared down at her, as unmoving as if he were growing from the earth itself. There was such an intensity in his face and in the tautness of his broad shoulders under the soft brown leather of his jacket that Lane couldn't tear her gaze from him. His eyes were almost angry, as she had expected them to be, but they held something else, too, an excitement and a mystery that she hadn't expected to see there.

Neither of them moved at all; his look and his nearness were creating a new, elemental world just for them, a world trembling with possibilities that dissolved her anger and left her waiting, existing only through her senses.

The crashing of the waterfall, the rosy yellow of

the morning light filtering among the trees, the sweet fragrance of the violets in her hands, became so sharp that she could hardly bear them.

He studied her, then turned his attention to the small blossoms in her hand. A moment later his dark eyes returned to her face, absorbing its every detail. They stopped at the sensual curves of her lips, and for a long breathless time they rested there. Her heart thudding, her balance gone, she wondered wildly whether he was going to kiss her.

Then, suddenly, he crouched down and in one flowing gesture broke off one of the diminutive blossoms and tucked it into the honey-colored braid above her ear. His fingers brushed her temple as he threaded the stem through her hair, and when the flower was secure he traced a path down through the escaping tendrils in front of her ear, his touch as delicate as the hazy spring light that enclosed the two of them.

The feel of his hand against her sensitive skin flowed through her and left her powerless. She couldn't speak; she couldn't take her eyes from his; she could hardly breathe. She wanted nothing, nothing at all, except to understand who this man was, what this magic was that existed between them.

His eyes held hers for another long moment, then he was gone among the trees.

Lane didn't move. She knelt, looking after him, still holding her little bouquet. The crunching of his footsteps on the leaves and twigs scattered across the rough ground floated back to her through the morning air.

Who could he possibly be? she wondered. How could he make her feel this way? How could a man she'd never seen before give her the feeling that he could touch her very soul just by looking into her eyes?

The dampness of the dewy earth soaked through the heavy denim at last, and the cold on her knees brought her to her feet. She brushed at her legs, then wandered slowly over to the rock where the man had been when he first spoke to her.

She leaned against its smooth edge and looked unseeingly out over the valley. Her beloved hills were still there; the waterfall was still speaking to her; she was still surrounded by the trees she loved, but now there was an emptiness, a loss of something she couldn't name, something she hadn't known existed when she'd climbed to this spot a few minutes earlier. That extraordinary clarity that had entered all her senses was gone.

Finally she pulled the tiny yellow flower from her hair and twirled it abstractedly in her fingers as she began the walk back down the mountain, her mind still filled with the image of his face looking down into hers, her body still vibrating from the power of his touch.

Voices reached her as she climbed the steps and crossed the back porch to Alice's kitchen.

"I *am* going to graduate, Aunt Alice," Rowena was saying testily. "After all, I could have quit school and gone to New York last year, but I didn't."

Alice thumped the black iron skillet angrily on the burner as Lane opened the door. "Well, if you had, you'd have starved last year instead of this one, then," she retorted sharply. "You have no business leaving home until you can take care of yourself."

"I *can* take care of myself," Rowena answered, rattling the silverware as she set the table. "I can get a job. . . ."

Alice frowned and opened her mouth to interrupt the girl, but before she could continue the argument Lane called out from the doorway. "Good morning," she said, including them both in her smile. "I'm so glad I didn't miss breakfast; I've had a long walk and I'm famished."

Alice returned the smile as she poured beaten eggs into the frying pan. "It'll be ready in a minute," she said. "We slept a little late, so you're right on time."

"Hi, Lane," Rowena muttered, obviously forcing herself to try to sound cheerful as she finished her task and returned to the counter. "Want some coffee?"

Lane picked up a mug and met her at the coffeepot. "Sounds great. It's still pretty chilly out there, even if it is spring," she responded.

As they sipped the coffee, leaning against the counter, Rowena's green eyes took in every detail of Lane's appearance—the smooth-fitting jeans, her long-sleeved cotton knit shirt under the blue and yellow patchwork vest and the braids that started at a center part and wound around her head.

"I really like your hair," she said at last.

"Thanks," Lane responded. "Yours would look good this way, too."

"I can never get the braids right in the front," Rowena said. "I can't hold them tight enough or something."

"I'll show you how," Lane offered. "This afternoon when I finish meeting my contact people, come up to my room and we'll practice if you want."

Rowena smiled for the first time since Lane had interrupted the argument with her aunt, and Lane had the sudden feeling that they could be friends. It might be almost like having a little sister.

"Great," the girl answered. She turned to Alice. "Are the eggs about done, Aunt Alice?" she asked. "I'm nearly late for school."

"I'm nearly late opening the shop, too," Alice replied testily, "but I aim to relax and eat my breakfast anyhow. You'd better just sit down now and eat yours, too, Rowena. You haven't eaten enough lately to keep a bird alive."

Rowena nodded and sighed in mock weariness as she and Lane helped the older woman carry the food to the table. "I know," she said tartly. "You've told me that before."

Alice gave her a sharp look as they sat down to steaming platters of eggs, bacon and buttermilk biscuits, and then she turned to Lane.

"Speaking of your contact people," she said, passing the strawberry jam she'd made, "I've thought of another one. He can introduce you to his granddaddy and some of the other old-timers." She helped herself to the ruby-colored preserves when Lane had finished. "Thad Campbell. He makes dulcimers and plays nearly every instrument there is, and his grandpa, Old Man Campbell, used to build log cabins and fireplaces, and he'll tell you hunting tales 'til the world looks level."

"Oh, he sounds perfect," Lane exclaimed. "I'll go see him soon, maybe tomorrow."

"He *is* perfect," Rowena assured Lane dreamily, sipping at her coffee.

Alice frowned at her again.

"He lives up on Bittercreek," the girl went on, ignoring Alice's glare, "but he has a little shop not too far from ours here in Covey."

Alice tried to take over the conversation. "He works at the shop most of the time instead of at home," she told Lane. "Quite a few tourists pass through Covey, and he gets orders for instruments from them."

"I'll take you to his shop," Rowena put in eagerly. "Let me know when you want to go see him."

"*I* can take her down there and introduce them," Alice stated firmly. "I don't want you hanging around Thad's shop flirting with him. He's way too old for you."

"He's twenty-six!" Rowena said, a pout forming on her expressive mouth. "I'll be eighteen next month, and he's twenty-six. I don't think he's too old for me."

"He is!" Alice retorted. "You ought to make up with Sam Lee, or go with some of the other boys your age."

"Oh, Aunt Alice!" Rowena groaned, shaking her head in a hopeless gesture and pushing back her chair. "I truly have to go now or I *will* be late." She carried her dishes to the sink and went to the door. "See you tonight," she said to Lane. She gave her aunt a wave. "'Bye, Aunt Alice. See you." And she was gone.

Alice shook her head. "She's a handful, that girl," she confided to Lane. "I've had her here since her mother died. She was only six then, so now she's just like my own." The frown creased her forehead again as she sipped her coffee. "I just hope I can do right by her," she said slowly. "I've got to keep her from going off to New York or some such place all by herself."

"Maybe she'll stay here, or somewhere nearby," Lane comforted her. "Lots of young people talk about going to the big city, but most of them never do."

"I hope she won't." Alice nodded, wrapping both hands around her coffee mug as if to warm them. "I want her to go to college. She could go to the one at Berea or to Cumberland College and still be fairly close to home."

"I could tell her the good things about college if that would help," Lane offered, going to the stove to get the coffeepot. She refilled her cup, and Alice held hers out for more.

"I'd like that, if you would," she said. "You've only been here a few days, but Rowena really admires you. I don't want her to be a bother to you, though."

"Oh, she won't be," Lane assured her. "I'm an only child, and I've always wanted some sisters and brothers. I'll just pretend that Rowena is my little sister for the time that I'm here."

Alice was clearly pleased. She smiled warmly and passed the plate of biscuits to Lane. "Have another one," she urged. "You need to build up your strength for climbing all over these hills."

"I don't want to be so fat I can't climb them, though." Lane laughed, succumbing to temptation. She bit into a tender biscuit dripping with butter and sweet jam. "This is heavenly, Alice!" she exclaimed. "I'm so glad your boarding house serves breakfast; I wish you had time to cook the other meals, too."

Alice smiled appreciatively. "Sometimes I wish so, too," she answered, "but I like running the shop."

"It puts you in contact with lots of people." Lane nodded. "You get to meet all the people who make the crafts you sell and the tourists who buy them, too."

Alice stood up and began stacking dishes. "I'd better get down there," she said. "Polly Clay told me she's bringing me three new quilts today and hers are some of the best."

Lane finished her coffee and stood, too. "I need to get busy," she said. "I'd like to talk to at least three contacts today if I can."

Together they cleared the table, and Alice started rinsing the dishes. Lane picked up the vest she'd hung on the back of her chair and started to her room.

"I never thought to ask how your walk was," Alice called over the sound of running water. "Did you find the waterfall?"

"Yes," Lane answered, stopping in the doorway. "It was gorgeous. . . ." The memory of the mysterious man and their intimate encounter had been hovering at the back of her mind and now it swept over her again. Wondering if Alice would know who he was, Lane thought of describing him to her, but before she could begin, the harsh ring of the phone echoed through the house.

"Would you answer that?" Alice asked. "My hands are all wet."

Lane nodded and went to the phone on the rickety wooden table in the wide hallway. The voice of her favorite professor responded to her "hello."

"Dr. Burroughs!" she said, delighted. "What are you doing awake and working so early? You know you never come in until noon!"

"You are impudent, as usual," he said, chuckling back at her. "I'm always working, night and day." He cleared his throat, a nervous habit that Lane had learned to ignore during the six courses she had taken from him. "But enough levity," he went on. "I'm calling to give you an assignment."

"Not something else," Lane answered, groaning. "You know I already have far more than I can do in the six months that my grant covers."

"It's not something new, it's about your grant," he told her. "I've just heard from Vance Morgan, the philanthropist who donated it to the university. It seems that he's leasing a house fairly near Covey and will be staying there for a while."

"What's he doing here?" Lane asked in surprise. "I thought he was from Chicago."

"He is, but evidently he has some business interests in Kentucky, so he's enjoying the scenery while he takes care of them. He's leasing a friend's summer home, he says, and it's on Lake Jackson, so I'm sure it's more pleasant than an office in the city at this time of year."

"Right," Lane said. "I've just come from a long walk and everything here is absolutely beautiful."

"Well, anyway, Lane," Dr. Burroughs went on, "I want you to go see him and thank him for the grant and his interest in the university. Just build up a rapport, all right?"

"All right," Lane said. "I'll be glad to."

"He's hinted to Dr. Elliott that he's interested in funding more grants and maybe even in establishing a large endowment for the department," the professor said, his voice very serious. "With budgets getting tighter all the time, we can't afford not to follow up on such an opportunity."

"I understand," Lane assured him cheerfully. "I'll be glad to tell him all I can about the department and my work. Did he tell you how to get to this house on the lake?"

"No, but he gave me a telephone number," Dr. Burroughs replied. "He said his secretary will give you directions when you call. Do you have a pencil and paper?"

Lane picked up the little pad beside the phone and wrote down the number he gave her, wondering all the while at the fact that Vance Morgan was staying nearby.

"That's it, then. Good-bye, Lane, and good luck with your findings," he said. "Call me if you have any questions." He cleared his throat again. "Let me know how the meeting with Morgan goes."

"I will, Dr. B., and thanks," she replied.

Lane hung up the phone and stood staring at it thoughtfully for a moment; then she picked it up again and dialed the number the professor had given her.

A professional secretary's smooth voice answered, and the woman efficiently made an appointment for Lane to come out the next afternoon. "I'm sure he'd like to see you," she told Lane, "and he'll be leaving Friday morning on a trip to New York for the weekend, so tomorrow would be best. Would four o'clock be convenient?"

"That will be fine," Lane answered, mentally rearranging her plans for the day. She picked up the pad again. "I'll need directions to the house, however."

She wrote down the directions and hung up just as Alice appeared.

"Oh, Alice . . ." she said, intending again to ask about the magnetic dark-haired man who kept coloring her thoughts, but Alice was taking her sweater from the curving coatrack with brisk efficiency and rummaging in her bag to see whether she'd forgotten anything.

"Yes?" the older woman queried absently.

"Oh, nothing," Lane answered with a smile. "I don't want to make you any later than you are. We can talk about it tonight."

"All right," Alice said, throwing the words back over her shoulder as she went out. "See you then."

"Good-bye, Alice; have a good day," Lane called after her. She stared at the leaded glass in the old oak door for a long moment, then pushed the dark-eyed man from her thoughts and began to concentrate on her work and Vance Morgan.
the pad again. "I'll need directions to the house, however."

Chapter Two

✻

Lane tried to check her appearance in the rearview mirror and keep an eye on the road at the same time, but she couldn't really do both. The highway was narrow and each curve seemed to wind back more sharply than the one before it. When there were no other cars in evidence she looked at her makeup again.

She hoped she didn't look too young. She ran her hand through the blond hair hanging loose to her shoulders and frowned at her reflection. Maybe she should have left it in braids or put it into a bun; after all, she wanted Vance Morgan to take her seriously, to feel that the money he had given to the university was being used by a professional.

She rubbed at the little bit of blusher that was smeared too low on her cheek, then turned her attention back to the road. She had dressed in too much of a hurry—her time had been limited ever since she'd made the mistake of stopping on the main street of Covey, where garrulous Jasper Cotton had waylaid her. It had been almost impossible to get away from him and his reminiscences ever since she'd met him. He had heard that she was interested in the way things used to be and he was making it his personal mission to tell her every detail of his days in the coal mines.

A patch of yellow flowers high on the hillside caught her eye, and suddenly the face of the mysterious man she'd met the day before came back into her mind. She could almost feel the touch of his fingers against her face and smell the mountain morning that they had shared. She might never see him again, but she would think of him every time she saw those violets. And maybe some other times, too, she admitted to herself, slowing down a little for a hairpin curve. The way he'd looked at her had touched something deep inside.

Her watch said five minutes to four when she turned off the highway onto the narrow gravel strip marked "Private Road" that led to Vance Morgan's temporary home. She followed it up the hill, and after almost half a mile it led her out of the trees and into a clearing that was dominated by a low-lying glass and cedar house sprawled along the top of the cliff. The afternoon sunlight reflected off the blue water of a large lake below.

Lane parked in a shaded area in front of the garage and looked at the house for a moment. Then she got out, smoothing her crisp blue linen slacks and matching silk blouse, and headed up the winding stone walkway.

The secretary with the satin voice opened the door and introduced herself as Mrs. Howard. "Mr.

Morgan is expecting you," she said when Lane gave her name. "Come this way, please."

Lane stepped into a wide foyer full of plants that were reaching toward the skylight above. The house seemed to stretch in all directions, its white walls and natural wood forming the perfect backdrop for the handmade baskets and primitive paintings that were hanging there.

She followed the secretary through the hallway into a spacious room that opened onto one of the redwood decks overlooking the lake. Several couches and easy chairs covered in earth-toned fabrics were tastefully arranged around handwoven rugs on the hardwood floor. The large light-colored wooden desk sitting unobtrusively in one corner and the bookshelves and tables scattered around the room were simple, almost Shaker-like in design.

"Please make yourself comfortable," Mrs. Howard said to Lane. "Mr. Morgan will be in soon."

Lane settled herself at one end of a long couch. She picked up a small carving of a deer that was on the table beside her and was looking at it when she heard the sliding door to the deck open.

A tall man stepped through it, his quick stride and broad shoulders somehow familiar. He closed the door and turned to greet her, and she looked up into the confident brown eyes of the man she'd met on the bluff.

A thrill of surprise and excitement shot through her. She'd found him again!

He crossed the room quickly and took her hand. His touch was firm and totally assured, and the magic she'd felt on the mountain was still there.

"I'm Vance Morgan," he said, his smile a slash

of white in his tanned face. "And you must be Lane Matthews. It seems we neglected to introduce ourselves yesterday."

At last Lane said inanely, "I had no idea who you were."

"Neither did I," he replied. "I mean, I knew who I was, but not who you were," he went on lightly, his smile deepening.

She tried to regain her composure as he pulled a chair around to face her. He settled into it and crossed one leg over the other knee.

"No wonder you don't want an amusement park in the mountains," he said, looking at her keenly. "If you're going around studying old folkways you naturally don't want things to change."

The mention of their disagreement intruded on her awareness of him, and the frustration she had felt at his cavalier attitude toward the land began to come back. He made her sound like some sort of reactionary stick-in-the-mud!

"Even if I weren't studying anything, I wouldn't want the mountains ruined just to make some greedy developer rich!" she replied, her tone a bit sharper than she had intended.

He raised one eyebrow wryly. "You're talking to the greedy developer who's building Greenbriar Amusement Park."

An icy feeling, anger mixed with fear and disappointment, streaked through her. "You?" she gasped. "You're the one who's bringing in those horrible yellow machines to tear up the mountainsides?" She stared at him incredulously. "But you can't be! You funded my grant. You have to be interested in the mountain culture and in this area."

Her wide blue eyes were glued to his, dark with confused emotions that were churning inside her. "How can you want to preserve all this and yet tear it down at the same time?"

"It's good to preserve the old ways in a museum," he replied mildly, "but it's insanity to try to keep them functioning in real life. There's no way to keep the mainstream of American culture out of the mountains."

"Do you call an amusement park culture?" she demanded scornfully, anger obscuring all her other feelings.

"Not at all," he answered smoothly. "I'm just saying that these days no group of people can remain isolated forever."

"I'm not saying they should remain isolated; I just don't want all this natural beauty ruined," she said hotly. "But you haven't answered my question. Did you give a grant to the university just so I could come down here and preserve samples of everything before you destroy it?"

He gave her a long look. "I'm not going to destroy it; it's already changing without any help from me."

He rose and with his self-assured stride went to his desk. He picked up a large piece of stiff cardboard, brought it back to the couch and held it out to her. Her hands shaking with anger, she took it and saw that it was a detailed architectural drawing entitled "Greenbriar Amusement Park."

"It was sort of a coincidence about your grant," he said in an explanatory tone. "I happened to be planning Greenbriar when I went to Midwestern's president, Dr. Elliott, to say that I'd like to make a contribution. He told me about your project, and it caught my interest immediately because it was located so near my own new one."

Lane moved her eyes from the hateful drawing in her hand to his face. He looked back at her calmly from his six feet of height, his stance, like his voice, filled with arrogant sureness. "I saw that I could make an advertising tie-in there; I could give something to the university and promote my own business at the same time."

"Advertising! The only purpose of this grant is to get cheap advertising for you, for your . . . your project to decimate the mountains?" Her voice was rising in spite of her efforts to remain calm.

"It's publicity, not cheap advertising," he answered quickly, stung to anger. "And that's not the only purpose of the grant. I think Midwestern is a great school, and I'm sure that what you're doing is important."

"Oh, really?" she shot back at him. "You sound as if you couldn't care less."

His jaw tightened, and his eyes went as hard as the mountains that waited so serenely outside the expanse of glass that surrounded them. "Look, Lane, I'm not doing a thing to this land or to these people that someone isn't going to do sooner or later, and in the process I'm bringing them employment and recreation." His hard gaze bored into her as he continued, "So don't sit here and tell me that what I'm doing is bad."

"It *is* bad," she cried, "and you can't see that because you're so ignorant about these people." She rose to face him, straightening to her full five feet seven inches, her blue eyes blazing into his almost black ones. "You're a total outsider coming in here all set to play God!"

He continued to look at her for an endless moment; then with arrogant deliberateness he took the drawing from her trembling fingers and strolled over to stand in front of the massive birchwood desk. "I'm not playing God and I'm not playing the villain, either," he said, his voice low and infuriatingly inflexible. "I wanted to contribute to the work that's being done at Midwestern and if it happens that one of my philanthropies can be used to benefit one of my business investments, so much the better."

Casually he tossed the posterboard onto the shining wood of the desk. "It also happens that in the process I'll be doing a lot of good for this community. If you'll open your eyes and look around objectively, you'll see that it needs all the help it can get."

The harshness of his tone made the color drain from her face. She stared at him, a chill shooting through her at the implacability of his tone and his words. "You're the one who can't be objective," she said. "You can't make *any* kind of judgment because all you can see is the outside. You can't get close enough to anyone in this community to see what it's really like!"

She stood staring back at him, silently challenging him. Smothering feelings surged stronger and stronger inside her: frustration and anger at his unbending attitude; fear of the effects of his power; and even now, furious as she was, an awareness of his virility, that masculine magnetism she hadn't been able to put out of her mind since they had met. What a fool she had been to wish she could see him again!

She tried to maintain some kind of control over

the maelstrom inside her as she searched his face for a hint of insight into his mind, for a trace of the understanding he'd seemed to have of her on the bluff the day before. How could those glinting dark eyes be so hard and dispassionate today, when they had been so mysteriously perceptive of her then? Surely he couldn't really be so totally impervious to her feelings and to those of the people whose land he was invading!

His deep voice broke into her thoughts. "Think about it, Lane," he said, "and you'll see things differently. You're all safe in the cocoon of graduate school now, but as soon as you finish and get out into the world you'll have to see reality."

"Don't insult me, Mr. Morgan," she replied, flinging the glacial words like sleet against the rock-hard cragginess of his face. "You're the one who's in a cocoon. You're so wrapped up in a blind chase after more and more money that you can't see that there are other, more important things in the world!"

Without giving him a chance to reply she turned and left the room.

Startled by the whistling of Alice's teakettle floating up the narrow stairs from the kitchen, Lane came instantly awake. Tiredly she pushed her tousled hair out of her face and kicked the wrinkled sheet and patchwork quilt off her legs. She sighed and rubbed her eyes, trying without success to take away the grainy, exhausted feeling that had grown progressively worse as the interminable hours of the night had dragged on.

Squinting, she peered at the clock on the small pine table beside her bed. It was a gesture that was second nature, a movement that she must have made a hundred times since she'd forced herself to go to bed at midnight. The round, bland face of the clock assured her unsympathetically that it was indeed morning.

In another now habitual gesture, she wadded her thin feather pillow into a ball at her back and scooted up to sit against the tall wooden headboard of the old-fashioned bed. All night she had assumed that if she sat up straight she would be able to think straight, but that hadn't proved true yet.

She had been over and over it in the hours that had passed since she'd walked out of Vance Morgan's house in a daze, but her thoughts were still a disorganized jumble. She was very fond of Dr. Burroughs, and she would love to help him and her school as well, but he would just have to find some other way to encourage Vance Morgan's interest in Midwestern. She hadn't even been able to thank him for her grant, they had been at each other's throats so quickly. No, she wouldn't discuss that or anything else with the man; in fact, she hoped she never had to see him again.

Fleetingly, illogically, that thought brought with it an image of Vance's square, tanned face and his eyes, thoughtful and darkly searching, as they had been in the early morning haze on the mountainside. It was an image that had come to her more than once during the hours when she had tried to sleep, the hours that she had spent wondering how the experience of the afternoon could have upset her so much.

Restlessly she swung her long legs over the edge of the bed and felt around on the braided rug for her wooden clogs. She slipped her feet into them and walked to the paned window on the east side of the room. She pulled the thin curtain aside so that she could look out at the mountain landscape she loved, but this morning even the tree-covered hillsides were no comfort.

Wearily she leaned her forehead against the cool glass. It was still very early, and light was just filtering through the narrow gaps and valleys from a sun that was hidden by the mountains.

Lane could hear the faint morning chatter of the birds. When she raised the window, the air that drifted in was weighted with the mysterious mixture of scents that came from the hundreds of varieties of plants that the hills had preserved for centuries. She took several very deep breaths; the fresh air already held a promise of summerlike heat.

Without warning she was caught up again in the magic and the solace that the mountains had always held for her, the feeling of stability and permanence that had been missing in her life until the first time she had come to them to stay.

As she absorbed the panorama outside the tall, narrow window, she knew suddenly that she was tied even more tightly to this place than she had realized before. This irreplaceable morning and the infuriating confrontation with Vance Morgan had made her see that.

How could anyone not feel the same way she did about this nurturing land? How could a man as intelligent as Vance Morgan escape its seduction?

With a last loving look at the green land that seemed close enough to touch, Lane turned and went swiftly to the plain pine armoire that served as the room's only closet. She took out a fresh pair of faded jeans and a buttercup yellow cotton shirt with short sleeves, appropriate for the promise of heat that was in the air; then she went to the old chest of drawers that matched the bed for her underthings.

She headed for the tiny bathroom down the hall, her mind working clearly for the first time since the devastating meeting at the house on the lake. There had to be a way to make him see all this the way she did. If only he could get to know the people and the land, maybe it would lessen the damage he would do.

"Hi, Lane," a bright voice called on Monday afternoon. "Wait and I'll walk with you."

Lane turned to find Rowena swinging down from the steps of the school bus that was bringing her back to Covey from the county high school.

"Are you going to the shop?" Rowena asked as she caught up to Lane on the narrow main street.

"Yes. I want your aunt to introduce me to Thad Campbell," Lane answered, "and at this time of day I thought maybe she'd have the time."

"Oh, I'll take you to see Thad," Rowena assured her. "No need to bother Aunt Alice with that."

Lane gave her a knowing smile. "I thought you all settled that the other day at breakfast," she said. "I think we should at least tell Alice where we're going."

Rowena looked at her quickly with a sideways glance from underneath her long lashes. She pretended to pout a little; then at last she shrugged.

"Oh, all right," she said. She shifted her books to her other arm and, with a sigh, led the way into Alice MacDonald's rustic shop.

Alice was at the back of the large room, teetering precariously on a short stepladder. Her arms were full of a brightly-colored appliquéd quilt, which she was struggling to drape over a railing fastened high on the wall.

"What're you doing, Aunt Alice? Are you trying to take over my job?" Rowena asked teasingly. "I thought you always left the climbing to me."

"I usually do, honey," the older woman answered as she turned awkwardly to greet them. "But I didn't think I had time to wait today—there's a busload of people due into town any minute now, a group from Louisville down here on a tour to see the dogwood in bloom."

She turned back to her work, continuing to talk over her shoulder. "Polly's quilts are always big sellers, and I want to get them all on display before the tourists come in."

"Then you won't have time to go with me," Lane remarked, putting her small shoulder bag on the counter and beginning to look around the room intently. There were always new additions to the handmade items that Alice sold for the mountain artisans, and she didn't want to miss any of them.

Rowena slipped onto the tall swivel stool behind the cash register and gave it a whirl. "I told her you don't need to go with her anyhow," she told her aunt in her most pleasant tones. "I can go."

Alice finished with the quilt, climbed down the ladder and stepped back into the room to judge the effect. "Go where?" she asked distractedly.

"Up to Thad Campbell's place," Lane said. "I've tape-recorded stories about one-room schoolhouses all day, and I'm tired of talk. I'm about ready for some music."

Alice gave no indication that she'd heard the answer to her question. "Do y'all think I should leave the Flower Basket one there, or would it look better to put the Double Wedding Ring in the middle?" she asked, her eyes never leaving the colorful, intricately patterned quilts unfurled against the natural wood of her back wall.

Lane walked over to stand beside her landlady, where she could get a better view of the vivid bedcovers. "Leave it there," she advised. "The others are patchwork and it isn't, so they balance each other, plus the yellows and greens in it pull the colors in the other two together."

Alice gave her a big smile. "I knew there must have been a reason why I chose it for the middle to begin with, but I had no idea what it was," she said. She turned to her niece. "All right, that's settled," she said briskly. "Now, what's this about Thad Campbell?"

"We just came by to say that we're on our way to see him," Rowena replied.

Alice chuckled. "Rowena, you do beat all," she said. "You never give up."

"I didn't do anything," Rowena protested. "Lane's the one who said she was going to see Thad, and I just offered to go along."

"Well, all right, this once," Alice said. "But, Rowena, you remember that Thad is a whole lot closer to Lane's age than he is to yours."

"I will," the girl answered petulantly, sliding off the stool and coming around the counter to Lane. "Let's go."

As Rowena walked beside Lane along the tilting sidewalks of Covey, she giggled. "Aunt Alice will be in a fit now until we get back," she said. "She thinks I'm going down here to ask Thad for a date or something."

"Well, are you?" Lane teased.

"No," her companion replied, giggling again. "I'm not quite as forward as she thinks I am." She waved at a dark-haired girl who was coming out of a store across the street. "Thad's got a mind of his own, anyway," she mused, almost to herself. "He's not like Sam Lee or any of the other boys I know."

They walked the equivalent of about two blocks, although there were no side streets to mark them. The town, like so many others in the mountains, was long and narrow, fitting itself into the natural valley formed by the ever-present creek; there was room for only one main thoroughfare. When Lane had first come to the Cumberlands, it had seemed strange to her that so many of the towns were made up of just one long street, but now she no longer noticed it.

Thad Campbell's shop was on the opposite side of the street from Alice's, and as Lane and Rowena crossed over to it they could hear the lively sounds of the old dance tune, "Cripple Creek," being played energetically and with a great deal of skill. They entered to find five men gathered in the center of the room, two with fiddles, one with a bass, one with a rhythm guitar and one with a dobro, tapping their feet and nodding their heads in time to the music.

The musicians were so absorbed that they hardly acknowledged Rowena and Lane, who stood uncertainly for a moment and then accepted the silent invitation of a genial old man to come sit beside him on a long bench just inside the doorway. When the tune was finished, the band immediately swung into "The Orange Blossom Special."

"That's Thad," Rowena whispered to Lane. "The good-looking fiddler with the beard."

Lane had already decided that he must be the man that Rowena had characterized as "perfect." He wasn't tremendously handsome; he was of medium height and his build was more wiry than muscular, but there was a volatile, passionate spirit in his movements, in his hazel eyes and, most of all, in his music, which could well be too much for a girl of Rowena's age. Watching him and listening to him, Lane understood Alice's concern.

They finished playing with one final flourish and began putting away their instruments. Thad walked over to the workbench that ran along one side of the room and laid his instrument carefully in its case. Then he turned to Lane and Rowena.

"Hi," he said, smiling broadly. "How come you all didn't make old Joe here dance with you? That's dancin' music." He ran one hand through his curling, sandy-colored hair in a gesture quick with nervous energy.

"I know. I could hardly sit still," Lane answered, returning his smile.

"They was fightin' over who'd git to dance with me first," the old man drawled, "and before they could decide, the music was over."

Rowena patted his hand affectionately. "That's right, Uncle Joe," she said with a laugh. "I'm determined that none of the other girls will beat my time with you."

The other musicians began calling their good-byes, so Joe added his farewells and shambled out after them. Lane wandered over to the workbench, where there were several dulcimers in all stages of completion, and Rowena followed her while Thad went with his guests to the door. When everyone was gone, he rejoined them.

"I like all the mountain music and I loved your band just now," Lane told him, "but dulcimer music is absolutely my favorite."

Thad beamed at her. "Rowena," he said, glancing toward the red-haired girl, "this is a lady after my own heart. Why don't you introduce us?"

Lane felt Rowena stiffen at his words, but the girl's voice was as light and cheery as it had been before as she made the introductions. "Lane, this is Thad Campbell, mountain mischief, I mean, music maker. Thad, this is Lane Matthews, who's doing some research about folkways."

Thad grinned at Rowena, and his amber eyes flashed into her green ones again for a moment in appreciation of her teasing, but then they came back to Lane's heart-shaped face and lingered there.

"A dulcimer lover," he said thoughtfully, "and researching the old ways. I think we're going to have a lot to talk about."

Once more Lane could feel Rowena's discomfort. "Rowena tells me that you know all the old-timers in the county," she replied, trying to include the girl in the conversation.

"I reckon that's about right," he affirmed, giving Rowena a quick nod. She smiled at him brightly before he turned his attention back to Lane. "Do you want to meet some of them?"

"Yes, and I want to tape as many of them as I can," she answered.

"Then you need to go with me to Junior Keaton's place Sunday," he told her, his hazel eyes sparkling. "My granddad and some of his friends will be there, and you'll hear some of the really old songs, maybe some you've never heard performed before. They might even get started telling stories, too." He rubbed his beard thoughtfully. "If I was you, I wouldn't bring the tape recorder, though," he suggested mildly.

"I won't," she answered with a smile. "I know I'll have to get acquainted first."

Thad nodded approvingly and started to say something, but Rowena interrupted. "We'd better go now, Lane," she said. "Aunt Alice may need some help with those tourists from Louisville."

"Yeah, that's a good idea," Thad said. "I saw the bus pull up when I was sayin' good-bye to the boys." He gave Rowena a brotherly pat on the arm. "Why don't you run on and help Alice," he suggested, "and let me show Lane some of my dulcimers before that crowd gets all the way up here?"

Rowena hesitated, obviously reluctant to leave without Lane, but unable to think of a way to get out of the situation. "Well, all right," she said at last. She turned the full force of her green eyes on Thad. "Good-bye, Thad," she said sweetly. "See you soon."

"'Bye, Rowena," he answered.

Rowena walked toward the door, then turned around and came back. "Lane, are you coming back to the shop before you go home?" she asked.

"Yes. I'll be there in a few minutes," Lane said, and Rowena flashed her a worried smile, then left.

"She's a good kid," Thad remarked casually as the door closed behind the girl.

He picked up one of the dulcimers, its top still held on with clamps, and showed it to Lane. They were talking about the cherry wood he'd used in it when a group of women, obviously tourists, swarmed in the door, chattering loudly and exclaiming over the varieties of musical instruments arranged in the small display window.

"I'll go so you can wait on your customers," Lane said.

"All right," he replied. "I'll call you soon to make plans for the musical."

"I'm staying at Alice's," Lane told him.

"I know," he said, walking with her to the door. "Now, don't forget that we have plans for Sunday."

"I won't," she called back to him from the street, marveling again at how people in the mountains always knew everything about newcomers even before they had met.

Lane walked back down the street at a leisurely pace, stopping to talk with a couple of the people she'd gotten to know since she'd been in Covey. By the time she arrived at Alice's shop the last of the tourists were leaving.

"You just missed the rush," Alice told her. "Seems like we sold half the goods in the store in the last hour."

"Well, at least you had a helper for part of the time," Lane said, looking at Rowena, who was hunched up on the high swivel stool, her chin in her hands.

"Yes, I couldn't believe she came back to help

her old auntie instead of staying to make eyes at Thad Campbell," Alice teased.

Rowena sat mute, pouting.

"She did, though," Lane said. "And she thought of it herself." She didn't add that Rowena's idea had been that Lane would go back to the shop with her.

"Well, I might as well have been down here helping you all the time," Rowena complained. "Thad couldn't see anybody but Lane." She looked directly at Lane, her green eyes clouded with disappointment and a hint of jealousy.

"Well, as you may recall, I reminded you that he's closer to her age than to yours," Alice said tartly. "However," she raised her gray eyebrows as she realized what Rowena was saying, "I don't intend for either one of my girls to be going with him. That's one of the wildest boys for miles around."

Lane smiled to herself at the revelation that she was now considered one of Alice's girls.

"He's already asked her to a musical," Rowena announced. "One of your girls is *already* going with him." She smiled bitterly at Alice. "And besides, you just now called him a boy," she said triumphantly. "Why don't you tell Lane he's too young for her?"

"I called him a boy because he's never grown up," Alice retorted, "and I doubt he ever will." She shook her finger in Rowena's gloomy face. "He's never grown up, but even so, he's too old for you, missy. And Lane isn't going with him, she's just doing her job."

"Don't worry, Rowena, Thad isn't really my type," Lane said cheerfully.

"Well, then, I'd like to know who is," Rowena said grumpily. "All the women like Thad."

"Oh, I don't know," Lane replied lightly. "I like 'em tall and dark, I guess." Illogically, Vance Morgan's handsome face flashed into her mind as she spoke. She tried to force the image away.

Rowena and Alice continued talking, more about the tourists now than about Thad, and Lane wandered restlessly around the shop. She picked up a wooden toy, a little man on a handle who could be made to dance on a rhythmically vibrating board. She stared unseeingly into his tiny painted face as she mentally gave herself a firm lecture. Vance Morgan should be back from New York by now, and she ought to try again to talk to him. Not only had she not thanked him as Dr. Burroughs had asked her to, she had probably alienated him to the point that he would forget all about the new grants for Midwestern. Poor Dr. B. would be horrified.

Lane returned the small, loosely jointed man to his place on the shelf, arranging him carefully so that he sat with his legs jauntily crossed. She'd try to start all over again with Vance—after all, there was nothing to lose and everything to gain.

Chapter Three

The next morning, immediately after breakfast, Lane went to call. She had to make him understand, she thought, the words running through her mind over and over again as the phone in the lake house began to ring. After all, as she'd told herself at the shop, she had nothing to lose.

A slight shiver of apprehension followed that thought, but she shook it off. She couldn't lose her heart to him, no matter how physically magnetic he was. Since they couldn't even talk civilly for ten minutes, they would certainly never have a man-woman relationship!

Mrs. Howard answered in her usual silken tones.

"Mrs. Howard, this is Lane Matthews. I'd like to make an appointment to see Mr. Morgan today."

"Just a moment, please," the secretary replied.

Carefully Lane tried to keep her mind a blank as she waited. If she thought about all the strong feelings that Vance could arouse in her, her voice would start to shake.

"Lane!" Vance Morgan's low voice came on the line. Suddenly, inexplicably, she pictured him standing over her on the bluff in the early morning haze, his tall form outlined against the waterfall in the pale light.

He sounded relaxed and interested as he had that day on the mountain, and she had to force herself to listen to his words instead of reliving that scene.

"I'd like to see you today, too," he was saying. "Why don't we meet for lunch?"

She was totally taken aback. Lunch! The last time she'd seen him they had been furious with each other and now he was suggesting lunch together.

"Lane?" he asked.

"Y—yes, I'm here," she managed finally. "That would be fine."

"Good," he said. "How about The Woodfern? One o'clock?" He seemed perfectly confident that she would agree.

"All right," she answered.

"Shall we meet there, or would you like me to pick you up?" he asked.

"I'll meet you," she said firmly. She certainly didn't want this meeting turned into some sort of a date. The only kind of relationship she could ever have with this man was a professional one, and even *that* would be difficult.

"Fine," he answered cheerfully. "See you soon."

All morning Lane thought about the luncheon with Vance. She tried to decide which of her new contact people she wanted to meet during the next

few days and she went over some information
about old mining songs that she wanted to ask
about when she went with Thad to the musical on
Sunday, but Vance Morgan was filling up her mind
and she couldn't really concentrate. More and
more she found herself going over every detail of
the time she had spent with him, both on the
mountain before she'd known who he was and,
later, at his house.

Finally admitting that it was hopeless to try to
focus on anything else, she resigned herself to
doing nothing more demanding than deciding what
she would wear to The Woodfern. While she went
through her closet she consciously tried to analyze
the few clues she had to Vance Morgan's character.

If she only knew what approach to take, she
thought. She was sure she could at least get him
interested in learning about the Appalachian people, in seeing the richness of what they had instead
of thinking that "they need all the help they can
get."

She shuddered again at the thought of the earth-
moving machines tearing away at the forested
mountainsides. If only she could perform a miracle
and convince him to give up the whole project!

With that idea uppermost in her mind, she forgot
about clothes for the moment and sank onto her
bed, lost in thought. When she really thought
about what Vance's park and other businesses like
it could do to this place, it made her almost
physically sick, she realized, and her eyes fastened
unseeingly on the green world outside her window.

It was all because she had wanted desperately to
be deeply rooted somewhere that she had become
involved with this land and its strong people. It was

a truth that she usually avoided thinking about, but today she couldn't help herself. They were her professional interest, true, but they were more than that—they represented an emotional security to her.

The remark she had made to Alice the other day about being an only child was the understatement of the century, she thought. Not only did she have no brothers or sisters, she had practically grown up without parents, too. When she was a teenager she'd sometimes wished bitterly that she were an orphan so that at least she would have had a chance of being adopted by a loving family.

That probably wasn't fair to her parents, she admitted, absentmindedly tracing the patchwork pieces of the quilt spread over her bed. They had loved her; they just had never had time for her. Her father was a career serviceman, and her mother had dedicated her life to helping him reach his goals.

They had been so wrapped up in all the demands of his career and in moving him up in rank year after year that they had hardly even realized that Lane was real. She'd always felt that they didn't know she was a person with ideas and goals and likes and dislikes of her own—they'd seen her as a possession to be shuttled from one boarding school or camp to another.

And even when she did get to spend some time at home, home had never been in the same place twice. The constant moves had deprived her of close friends and of the security of having familiar surroundings and an extended family during her childhood. By the time she had been old enough to make her own choices, the grandparents she had barely known were dead, and her parents were more remote than ever.

She had gone to the Midwest to attend college and had found that sociology and anthropology captivated her. She hadn't thought about it at the time, but much later she supposed that she'd decided to go into them to try to find a place for herself in the larger family of man, since she couldn't do so in the nuclear family she'd been born into. Whether that was true or not, she'd loved her courses, and when she'd gone into the Appalachians for the first time to do research, she'd had an instinctive feeling that she'd come home at last.

She'd loved the inherent warmth of the people she'd met and the feeling she constantly had that they, their homes and their institutions had held their places forever and that none of them had changed very much during all that time. There was an elemental sameness, an eternal verity, about the mountains, an immovable quality that fulfilled and satisfied the emptiness in a lonely, searching twenty-year-old world traveler.

Her living arrangements then had been much like her present one, except that there had been no little-sister substitute. There'd been only a much-needed grandmother-substitute who'd insisted on being called Granny Belle. She and Lane had become very close, and they still were. They talked frequently, and Lane visited her at least every other month or so.

Granny had understood Lane's loneliness, and in her straightforward, unsentimental way she had shared a lifetime of insights and observations, gradually becoming the mother that Lane had never really had. By the end of that summer Lane, too, had had roots. She belonged in the mountains.

She had assumed since that time that she would always live in or near these mountains. As yet she had no job offers, but she had almost another year to go for her doctorate and she had never really considered any other possibility. She would teach sociology in a college or she would do research or *something* after she graduated so that she could be settled in a place she loved, a place where she felt secure.

She had found her safe haven at last, but now Vance Morgan and other men like him were going to come in and change it. All the feelings of permanence and stability would be gone; new people would be moving in and out, and finally it would be just like any other place.

She glanced at her watch, and the lateness of the hour made her try to shake away the haunting thoughts and force herself back to the present. It would take at least twenty minutes, maybe more, to reach the restaurant, which was part of a secluded resort. It wasn't very far from Covey—if you could travel in a straight line—but the narrow winding roads made for extremely slow driving, and she had learned to allow for that in all her plans.

Quickly she made her selections from the pine armoire and, after she'd spread them carefully on the bed, she went down the hall to the little bathroom. She tried to think only about cheerful, positive things as she showered and dressed, psyching herself up to influence Vance Morgan.

Standing as far back in the room as she could from the tilted oval mirror attached to the dresser, she could just barely see herself from head to toe. Her navy-and-white-striped cotton sweater had long sleeves that ended in wide ribbed bands around her wrists, and the tightness of the ribbing was echoed by the three-button ankle fastenings of her navy poplin slacks. Her hair was in her favorite style—neatly braided on the sides and loose in back. The whole effect was crisp and casual, and she hoped that her manner would be, too, as she talked with Vance.

She picked up her slim navy envelope bag and left her room, determined that she would make him see his new surroundings through her eyes.

Lane stood just inside the double frosted-glass doors of the restaurant for a moment; then the maître d' approached. He led her across the main dining room and out onto a small flagstone terrace that seemed to be suspended in air, so steep was the drop below it. Vance was sitting at a table in one corner, but he stood as she approached.

He greeted her cordially, almost gallantly, and she was struck by the sharp contrast between his current manner and the way he'd looked at her and spoken to her the last time they'd met. For some reason she could hardly stop looking at him.

They settled into the cushioned wicker chairs and he took a wine bottle from the cooler nearby. He picked up her glass and smiled warmly.

"As you see, I've chosen the wine," he said. "But I did refrain from ordering the food until you could express an opinion."

"I appreciate that," she replied dryly.

"I knew you'd have an opinion, because every time we meet you seem to be expounding passionately about one subject or another," he went on lightly, looking up from pouring her wine with a teasing glance. That glance and the warm tone of his voice somehow made them seem to be old friends.

Her heart lurched, and her pulse beat responded to his nearness. It was as if there were some elemental law that gave him the power to completely undo her; she could feel herself being drawn to him in spite of her decision to keep everything between them strictly business.

She forced her thoughts away from analyzing the details of his even, chiseled features and gave him a long straight look, her blue eyes searching his inscrutable dark ones. Did he think that lunch at a luxurious restaurant and a gallant, lighthearted manner could erase the seriousness of the differences between them? Was he thinking of this as a date, a purely social occasion, a chance to charm and entertain her?

"Did you think that if you could get me started on the subject of food I wouldn't 'expound' about anything more controversial?" she asked. Her tone was light, too, but there was an undercurrent of ironic seriousness.

He smiled directly into her eyes. "I must admit that it did cross my mind," he replied, just as the waiter appeared at his elbow.

The warmth of that smile took the hardness from his sensual mouth and touched his eyes, as well. It communicated a sudden charm that was completely different from any impression she'd had of him, and she felt her pulse quicken again in response to his warmth.

She smiled back at him. "I'll have the quiche,"

she said. Then, quickly, she added in a bantering tone, "And that's all I have to say on the subject."

Vance chuckled and ordered her quiche and a club sandwich for himself, then added salads for both of them. When the waiter had gone, he turned back to Lane.

"If you won't discuss the cuisine, then what are we going to talk about?" he asked in mock dismay.

His eyes were still sparkling mischievously, and Lane had an instantaneous desire to respond to him in kind so that they could keep the lightness and warmth between them. The sunlight had melted every remnant of the morning's fog, and the reflection of the light from the green of the new leaves seemed to make the day sparkle. It would be wonderful to just relax and let this be the social occasion that Vance seemed to be trying to make it—an idyllic afternoon on a mountaintop.

She looked down and toyed with the large white napkin that was folded at her place, then sipped her wine. It would be so much fun to just enjoy him, to forget about the chasm that separated the different ways they looked at the world, but it would also be as dangerous as stepping off the terrace they were sitting on. This man stirred unknown physical responses in her, and the mystery of him fascinated her, but he had to remain a fleeting fantasy in her life. There was no way he could ever be a real part of it.

Lane straightened in her chair and met his eyes. "We can talk about your new project and these mountain people," she said firmly. "That's the reason I asked to see you today."

He raised one black eyebrow and looked at her quizzically.

"The last time we met you made the remark that they need all the help they can get," she went on. "Evidently you know almost nothing at all about this area."

"I don't see that there's so much I need to know," he replied, his voice still pleasant but edged with annoyance. "I'm perfectly capable of directing the building of Greenbriar. It's my fourth amusement park."

"But it's your first in Appalachia," she said as the waiter returned and served their salads, "and if you'd get to know this land you'd be enriched in lots of ways besides money."

Her words brought a thoughtful look to his face, a turning inward for a moment that she didn't understand; then the dark eyes were on her once again.

"But being enriched in money is the purpose of being in business," he said flatly. "That holds true here just as it does in Chicago. Appalachia is no different from anyplace else."

She picked up her fork and absentmindedly began to eat, searching her mind for the words to make Vance see that she was right.

He followed her example; then after a moment he asked conversationally, "Do you like the salad?"

The dark green spinach leaves and homemade croutons were in a tart vinegar dressing that was unique to the well-known restaurant.

"Yes, I do," she answered distractedly, her mind still on the problem of making him understand. "This dressing is fabulous. It's one of my favorite things about The Woodfern."

"It's one of mine, too," Vance answered. He

took a sip of wine. "I'm glad you've decided to talk about the food after all," he went on smoothly. "That's much more appropriate for lunch on a sunny terrace than our former topic of conversation."

"But I haven't changed the subject," she said unhesitatingly. "I don't want to be rude, but I really do want you to understand."

Vance sighed resignedly, then picked up the wine bottle and refilled their glasses. "Lane," he said evenly and with exaggerated patience, as if he were dealing with a particularly difficult child, "you're young and you're in love with your work and you're seeing all this through wildly romantic eyes. Basically there's nothing different about these people except that they're twenty years behind the times."

"But there is!" she cried. "They have so much to share that the rest of the country has almost forgotten—they're self-reliant; they're strong; they're wise and ingenious, and we can all learn a lot from them about interdependence and the human spirit!"

She caught her breath, forcing herself to stop. He could make her feel more of everything, even anger, than anyone else she'd ever known. She felt herself on the edge of pouring out all the old hurts and reasons for her passion for the mountains, and she certainly couldn't do that. She couldn't possibly share that with *him!*

Her feelings were never this intense, she thought as she steadied her hand and took a sip of wine. Well, she was *not* going to let him know it. She wasn't going to spill her innermost thoughts, and she wasn't going to lose her temper this time, either.

Vance took a bread stick from the basket between them and broke it abruptly in his tanned fingers. "You're dreaming, Lane; you'll see that in a few years. *Nobody* fits that description anymore."

Lane's throat went tight with sudden, despairing tears, and she just looked at him, her eyes wide and dark with the emotions that were roiling inside her. She wanted to shout at him that he didn't know what he was talking about, but the finality of his tone told her more effectively than his words did that it was useless to continue the discussion.

His eyes were unreadable as they bored into hers, and he said nothing as the waiter arrived with her quiche and his sandwich.

Lane waited until the man had gone, then she spoke. She was under control now and she had an idea. Her voice strengthened as she looked back at him with an unwavering blue gaze. "Why don't you come with me sometime and meet some of these people?" she asked. "My words are never going to convince you, but your own experience might."

He took a sip of wine and looked into her eyes with the same magnetic power that she'd felt on the bluff. "I'd like that very much," he said seriously. Then he smiled that marvelous smile again, and his eyes glinted with humor. "I'd like to go anywhere with you—I rarely meet a beautiful woman who's so passionate about her beliefs."

A sharp excitement shot through Lane, a purely physical reaction to the content and tone of his words. She wanted to tell him that *she* rarely met a virile, attractive man who was so mystifying, but instead she murmured, "That would be fine."

"Good," Vance said briskly. "Then it's settled. As soon as I can make a break in my schedule we'll go exploring the past."

"I'm so glad," she replied with a smile suddenly brilliant with hope, a smile that held all her determination to share the magic of the mountains with him.

"Oh, Vance, I wanted to see you today for another reason, too. To thank you for my grant and your interest in Midwestern."

"You're quite welcome." He picked up a section of his thick sandwich. "Now, let's enjoy our lunch and talk about something else, like this incredible view."

The agreement and the attraction between them intensified the day; the heavy, moist air immediately seemed warmer, and Lane suddenly saw everything more clearly. The expanse of woods below and around them became infinite, pale green and brown dotted with dogwood trees, full of all the possibilities in the world.

The small pink and white dogwood blossoms stood out like lace against the background of purple and blue green bluffs in the distance; it was all a backdrop created for her, for the small, white-swathed table and the handsome man across from her.

He was wearing a casual, pale blue shirt that blended with the sky behind him and set off his dark good looks. Her eyes kept going back to the contrast between the pale blue silk and the tan of his neck, to the strength of his masculine features and the myriad expressions that came into his eyes as they talked.

They did talk about the view, and Lane told him about some of the most scenic spots in the area. They talked about his recent trip to New York, too, and a little bit about themselves and their backgrounds.

Finally she said, "I really must be going—I'm supposed to meet someone at Alice's shop at four o'clock."

"I'll walk you out," he replied and signaled to the waiter for the check.

The afternoon was the warmest of the spring so far, and the air had a balmy quality that always came with summer in the Cumberlands. It seemed to envelop them in a cocoon, to caress their skin everywhere it touched.

They walked down to the parking lot slowly, as if in an unspoken agreement to make their time together last as long as possible. The fragrance of the woods floated to them, and they savored it, talking a little about the different colored blossoms they could see near the path.

The path was a winding one; it descended narrow stone steps to the parking area below, and as it became steeper near the bottom Vance took Lane's arm to steady her.

His touch was galvanic. She felt a warmth rush through her veins just as it had done when he'd given her that intimate smile, when his teasing had reached out to her. This was insane, she thought, trying to get control of her senses. How could she feel this kind of response to him when they had such different attitudes about everything important, when he had every intention of destroying this world she loved?

They left the last of the steep steps for the pavement of the parking area and began to cross it toward Lane's jeep. They walked slowly with Vance making a few casual remarks about the way the guest houses and conference rooms of the resort blended into the rocks and trees of their setting. Lane murmured what she hoped were appropriate responses, but whenever she tried to come up with something to add she could think of nothing except the strong fingers that were searing her skin through the thin cotton of her sweater. A desire to feel his fingers on her bare skin stirred in her, and with it a desire to feel his smooth, tanned skin under her hands.

They reached her jeep, and Vance reached out to touch a flowering branch that was brushing the hood.

"Is this one of the dogwood trees you mentioned?" he asked.

"Yes, it is," Lane replied. She looked up into his dark eyes with a teasing smile and added, "That's very good for a city dude."

He smiled, too, and the look that had reached into the depths of her the first time she saw him returned to his eyes. He took both her arms and turned her toward him, and desire stirred in her, desire mixed with fear. He was too strong, too powerful; she couldn't keep her bearings when he was touching her.

"I've become aware of things like dogwood trees and yellow violets since I met you," he said, his voice warm and vibrant. "In fact, I've become aware of some other things, too."

His glance moved meaningfully down and then up the length of her, taking in her long legs, her tiny waist and generous breasts, pushing against the thin fabric of her sweater with the shallowness of her breathing.

The afternoon light was emphasizing the high cheekbones and hard angles of his face; she wanted to trace those rugged planes with the tips of her fingers, but she was powerless to move. The touch of his hands and the intimacy in his voice and his eyes were destroying all the nerves in her body; she knew that she wouldn't be able to stand if he released her.

Their eyes held for long, long moments, as if they were trying to see into each other's souls, as if they could erase their differences with silence, since they hadn't been able to do so with words.

"Your hair is made from the sunlight," he murmured, running his fingers through the thick strands and lifting them to shimmer in the breeze. "I've been thinking that all afternoon."

The desire to be closer was growing, becoming a living presence in the fragrant air between them. She couldn't take her eyes from his, and finally, just as she felt that she would have to move closer to him, he bent his head to hers.

He touched her lips with his, and they were as warm as his voice had been. He drew the sweetness from her lips gently; then he pulled away a little and with tiny kisses explored the outline of her mouth.

Without conscious thought, she reached up to hold him, to run her hand into the shining black hair at the back of his neck.

His lips took hers with passion then, and as they

crushed hers she felt the tip of his questing tongue. It was tracing the fullness of her lips, moving along them hungrily, asking for entry.

She answered with the touch of her own tongue, her lips falling apart and inviting him into the recesses of her mouth. He came in, and she was suspended in a moment out of time, a moment in which nothing was real for her except the enticement that sent desire shimmering through her like a shaft of light.

He pulled her tighter into his arms and pressed her to him as if they were one person, his long, muscular arms holding her as if he would never let her go, the hard length of his body melding them together.

She responded with a passion she hadn't known was in her, crushing her lips to his and meeting the sweetness of his tongue with a wanting that took her breath away and left her trembling for more.

He broke the kiss then, pulling his mouth from hers so that she gave a little moan of protest. He arched away from her slightly and brushed her hair back with one hand so that his lips could reach the sensitive area beneath her earlobe. His warm breath and the woodsy, masculine scent of his cologne filled her senses until she swayed with dizziness, and when his lips touched her skin and trailed a path of electrifying kisses down the side of her neck, she clung to him with helpless longing.

At last his lips left her skin and with their going she felt unimaginably forsaken. He seemed to sense that, and he held her very close again for a dreamy moment. Then he tilted her chin up so that he could look into her eyes.

"I think we can get to know each other, Lane,"

he said huskily. "You're going to see that I'm not so bad after all."

All the way back to Covey, Lane wondered whether he was right. How could she ever really know a man who one moment could make her shout at him in anger and the next make her tremble with his kiss?

Chapter Four

The discordant noises of stringed instruments being tuned and the pleasant sounds of friendly voices began floating up to Lane as soon as Thad pulled his pickup truck off the narrow graveled road and stopped. When they got out she saw that their vehicle was the last in a line of several parked along the edge of the road, and that there were others pulled in among the trees on the gently sloping hillside.

"Good heavens, Thad! What is this?" she exclaimed. "I thought we were going to somebody's house for a small gathering, but this must be a full-fledged outdoor concert!"

He grinned. "Not really. It's just a good place to play because it's sort of a natural bowl, and everybody turns out for a little entertainment. It's Junior Keaton's place, like I told you; his house is right over there." Lane glanced toward the modest frame house nestled into the side of the hill, but she saw no one there. Everyone seemed to be gathered in the little open valley below.

As they started down the steep slope, Thad swung both his fiddle case and dulcimer case into his left hand and with his right took Lane's arm. The gesture reminded her of Vance and their walk out of The Woodfern. A shaft of excitement shot through her as that scene began to replay itself in her mind as it had done a dozen times. She still didn't understand why that memory and that man had such a hold on her imagination. She had almost decided that she must be losing her mind, since one kiss had set her dreaming of him when she was awake *and* when she was asleep.

Thad guided her through the trees and around the rocks and broken branches on the ground. She heard the voices of the children who were darting in and out, calling to each other as they organized a game, and she heard Thad's voice telling her what to expect from the afternoon, but Vance's deep tones and the strong, warm pressure of his hand on her arm replaced the present, not only in her mind, but in her body, too. A sharp longing filled her, a desire to feel his touch again that flowed through her like a river.

As she and Thad came out of the trees and approached the group in the clearing she forced the confusion of feelings away and focused her attention on the several groups of musicians and the audience gathered at the bottom of the hill.

"I can't wait to meet everyone, especially your grandfather," she told him, determined to fix her mind on her work again and banish the unsettling desire to see Vance that had been haunting her. "He must be one of the most famous people in the county; I've heard about him ever since I came to stay at Alice's."

"Well, there he is," he answered, nodding toward two elderly men ensconced in lawn chairs under a large pine tree. "With his friend, Uncle Joe. I don't think either one of them has missed a music-making or a dance in the past fifty years."

"Oh, yes, I remember Uncle Joe from the other day at your shop," she said. "He's quite a character."

"So is Grandpa," Thad said. "They make a pair."

Before they could go over to the two old men, one of Thad's band members welcomed them. "Here's Thad," he announced loudly. "Now I reckon we can finish tuning up and make some music." Lane recognized him as the man who'd been playing the bass when she visited Thad's shop. He was rotund and dark-haired, with a booming voice.

"Oh, you all just go on ahead without me," Thad replied. He turned to give Lane his impish smile and raised his voice so everyone could hear. "I'll be too busy to play today; I'm gonna take care of Lane here and let you all do the work."

"Oooh, no, you ain't," Junior answered firmly. "She couldn't stand a whole afternoon of nobody but you. *We'll* talk to her while *you* fiddle."

Good-natured laughter greeted this remark and all eyes turned to Lane. Thad introduced her to the musicians who surrounded her as he told them a little bit about her interests and her research. Then he led her over to some of their wives, who were arranging folding chairs, and, in spite of what he had just said, went back to the band to begin the tuning-up process.

Lane was preparing to sit beside Junior's wife, Katie, when she noticed Rowena standing nearby with another girl about her own age.

"Rowena, hi!" Lane said, going over to her. "I didn't know you were here."

"I knew *you* were," the girl replied, her green eyes dark. "No one could miss you—you seem to be the belle of the ball."

Thad's words came back to Lane, and she realized how they must have sounded to Rowena. "Oh, Thad was just teasing," Lane told her quickly. She went on with a bright smile, "He'd never give up playing to talk to me."

Rowena didn't reply, and Lane rushed on, trying to reassure her. "I don't think any girl could compete with music as far as Thad's concerned."

"Sounds like you know him pretty well," Rowena answered in a flat voice.

Lane hardly knew how to respond. This was a different Rowena, one with none of the playfulness that usually accompanied her remarks about the crush she had on Thad.

She really is crazy about him, Lane thought. She's truly serious about him! And she thinks I'm about to get him interested in me right when she's finally getting old enough for him.

A terrible sinking feeling accompanied Lane's realization. This would have to happen just when they were getting to be friends!

She answered quickly, keeping her tone light. "No, I don't." She tried to feel her way back to the friendliness that had been developing between her and Rowena. "I really don't know him at all; he's just trying to help me do my job."

"That's nice."

"Rowena," Lane began earnestly, "it isn't a surprise to you that I came here with Thad—"

The girl interrupted her. "Lane, I'd like you to meet my cousin, Janie Cowan," she said tensely.

Lane chatted with the girls for a few minutes, but the uncomfortable tension remained in the air. They didn't ask her to join them, and finally she went back to sit beside Katie as Thad scraped his bow across his fiddle and the music began.

The first selection was the ancient dance tune "Old Joe Clark," and within minutes it had wiped all thoughts of Rowena and her problems from Lane's mind. She felt herself smiling and tapping her feet at the sheer liveliness of it.

Not only was the spirit of the tune infectious, but so were the skill and enthusiasm of Thad's band. The music seemed to fill their bodies as well as the air around them, and it took Lane into its spell.

As soon as that tune was over they swung into "Shady Grove." Lane smiled at Thad and Katie and gave herself over completely to the music and the sunny afternoon. She leaned back and let the wind ruffle her hair and her mind float free.

Immediately it wandered to Vance. If he were there he would have been able to experience a little of what she had been trying to tell him. Then the day would truly have been perfect.

She opened her eyes and shook the hair away from her face abruptly as the significance of that idea penetrated her consciousness. She had to stop this!

Vance had never been very far from her thoughts since she'd left him standing beside the little dogwood tree at The Woodfern. She'd jumped every time the phone rang and had half-expected him to appear around every corner she turned in Covey.

She'd been trying to put her finger on the fascination he held for her, comparing him to Eric Watson, a man she dated at Midwestern. She barely knew him, but he could arouse feelings in her that Eric never could.

During college she had dated fairly frequently, and had had two serious relationships, the latter with Eric. He was counting the months until she would be back on campus at Midwestern, planning all the while to try again to convince her to marry him. Suddenly Eric seemed very far away, almost on another planet.

Trying to force Vance's image away, she turned to Katie. They began a low conversation as Thad and the group stopped to confer about their choices of songs, but always in the back of Lane's mind hovered the wish that this had been one of the "explorations of the past" that Vance had agreed to share with her. The music was stirring a restlessness in her that called out for him.

The musicians talked for a moment longer, then Thad called to another group to come and take a turn at making the music. He put his fiddle into its case and came to crouch beside Lane's chair.

"Let's go over and get acquainted with Charlie," he suggested. "We can listen to Wayne and his band and talk at the same time."

Lane smiled her assent and they moved over to

the old men under the tree, Thad again crouching down and Lane sitting on a handy rock to speak to them.

"Grandpa, Uncle Joe, this is Lane Matthews. She's visiting in Covey for a while."

Old Man Charlie pushed back his battered hat and tilted his head to look up at her, his clear blue eyes shrewd and friendly. "Pleased to meet you," he said. "Hope you enjoy your stay." He paused to rearrange the tobacco in his jaw. "You have any trouble with this boy here, jist let me know."

Lane chuckled. "I will," she promised.

"Oh, go on with you, Charlie. She ain't visitin' Covey to court your grandboy, she's a'studyin' the old ways," Uncle Joe announced importantly. "She's from a big university." He paused to squint at her carefully. "Ain't that right? Ain't you the pretty gal I seen down at Thad's shop?"

"Yes," she admitted with a smile.

"Old ways, huh?" Charlie repeated, mock sorrow in his voice. "I was about to git my hopes up that Thad finally had him a serious girl. I can't recollect when he's brought one of the girls he was courtin' to see me."

"I know yore eyes is failin' you, Old Man, but even you oughtta see that this gal is way too pretty for that rascal Thad," Joe teased.

"Wal, I can allus hope," Charlie asserted, pushing at the tobacco until it formed a large bulge in one jaw.

"So can I," Thad said quickly, flashing a smile at Lane. "But I have to admit that right now she's more interested in you than in me, Old Man. I told her you're the best chimney mason in East Kentucky and that you live in a cabin that was built by *your* grandpa, and from then on all she wanted to talk about was you."

The old man tilted his head and looked into her eyes again for a long moment, as if he were trying to divine what her real purpose was and to decide whether she could be trusted with his secrets. Lane looked back at him, fascinated by the steady clearness of his gaze.

"Wal, leastways you come in here to learn somethin' and not jist to see how much you could cheat us out of," he judged. "Most outsiders we see is here to git the shirts off'n' our backs."

"I'm not," she assured him. "All I want is to try to preserve some of the skills and stories that are about to be lost."

"Preserve 'em, huh?" He squinted at her and spat tobacco juice into the trees. "I've got a story. . . ." His voice trailed off, and he sat deep in thought for a long moment. At last he nodded and straightened briskly in his chair. "Come up the holler with Thad sometime," he invited. "I'll show you how they built houses so's they'd last."

After he'd issued the invitation Charlie pulled his hat down over his eyes again and went back into his thoughts. Lane and Thad bantered with Uncle Joe for a few more minutes, then they left the old men together.

"Old Man likes you," Thad told her as they walked back toward the band. "I can't recall him ever asking a stranger up to the hollow the first time they met. He's real private."

"I really like him, too," she answered. "Something in his eyes just speaks to me, but I can't put a name to it."

He nodded. "His cabin is really something," he

went on. "His granddad and *his* dad built it when his granddad was about twelve or thirteen, and that's where Old Man Charlie has lived all his life. They used dovetail notches and they fit like they'd grown that way."

Lane smiled in reply, but her mind was still more on the old man than on his cabin and her work. "Thad, what should I call him? You call him 'Grandpa' and 'Old Man,' and I hear everyone else say 'Charlie' or 'Old Man Campbell.'"

"Oh, whatever you like. He's known all over the county as 'Old Man Charlie Campbell,' and he answers to any part of it."

"That look in his eyes is as mischievous as a five-year-old's and at the same time as wise as if he were a hundred."

Thad chuckled and nodded agreement. "He's really closer to eighty than to either one of those ages, I think. He still works, too; he still helps build chimneys sometimes. He can make one draw every time."

"I don't doubt it," she replied. "I have a feeling that he can do a lot of things."

Thad settled Lane back into her chair beside Katie, then rejoined his band, who were about to play again. This time he picked up a dulcimer instead of his fiddle, and the crowd settled down into an almost silence.

Instead of the lively dance tunes he'd played before, he chose the plaintive, haunting melodies that the mountain folk had used for centuries to tell of their sorrows. As he played, the other instruments blending softly in the background in a way that brought to mind heartbreak and loneliness, he began to sing. He sang for over an hour, with even the children gradually gathering around to sit quietly and listen.

There was a sense of closeness drawing the audience together now, an experience shared by the old people and the young ones that bound them to each other and to the musicians in a way that was almost visible.

Lane shivered a little and rubbed at the goose bumps that had suddenly appeared on her arms. That kind of thing was very rare nowadays, she thought. In the cities that afternoon the old people were probably watching television and the younger ones were playing video games in the shopping malls.

And soon those video games and some carnival rides and who knew what else would be there in the mountains, right there in Covey. Just as soon as Vance could get Greenbriar open!

The thought jolted her completely out of the mood she was in, and her heart twisted painfully. *That* was what she needed to remember about Vance Morgan—the fact that he was there to build Greenbriar. Instead of remembering the way she melted when he kissed her, she needed to think about the way she would hurt when he destroyed her world, the only world in which she'd ever put down any roots.

Finally Thad looked around for his case and carefully laid the dulcimer in it. "Let's go home, boys," he suggested, his voice hoarse from singing. "That's all I've got in me for today."

"But, Thad," Rowena's lilting voice protested, "you can't quit now, you've got me crying."

He picked up his instruments and turned to her, stopping to ruffle her hair where she and Janie sat on the ground near the performers. "Just stay right where you are, kid," he said. "Ol' Wayne and his boys'll have you all cheered up in just a minute."

He didn't look into Rowena's face, but Lane did, and the expression she saw there confirmed the thought she'd had earlier in the day. Disappointment, frustration and longing all were mingled in the girl's frown and the set of her pouting mouth as she glanced quickly at the ground.

Thad came over to Lane and spoke softly. "You ready to go now?" She rose quickly to leave with him. She said good-bye to Katie and waved to Uncle Joe and Old Man, then began to walk around the edge of the crowd to reach the side of the hill where they'd left the truck. Rowena's eyes were on them the whole way, and when Thad took Lane's arm again as they began to climb the hill, they burned into Lane's back until she and Thad were hidden by the trees.

The next afternoon, when Lane arrived at Alice's shop, Rowena was still subdued, and her tone was guarded, even in her surprise.

"Lane! You're early. Aunt Alice said you'd be here to relieve me at three o'clock."

"I did tell Alice I wouldn't be able to come any sooner than three o'clock," Lane answered, "but I was over at Foggy Creek listening to Delcie White's memories of eight years in the one-room county school, and all of a sudden I just couldn't take it anymore. It seemed that the whole eight years were passing second by second while I sat there listening to her drone. Finally I said I had an appointment and practically ran out of there."

Rowena smiled almost against her will as she

began gathering her purse and books. "I can see why. I don't know how you managed to pick Delcie to interview in the first place. She talks slower than anybody I've ever known."

"And it *would* be the first true sleepy summery day this year," Lane went on. "I have a terrible case of spring fever. All I want to do is disappear into the woods, stretch out on a bed of pine needles and spend the whole afternoon looking up at the sky."

She blew a wisp of hair from her eyes as she went around behind the counter to put away the large leather tote bag that was her combination purse and carrying case for maps, directions and notes, plus her small tape recorder.

"I know," Rowena agreed. "That thought crossed my mind, too, but I have to go see a college counselor instead." She crossed the room to the door. "What a waste," she went on grouchily. "I'm not going to go to college unless Aunt Alice makes me."

"Maybe you'll change your mind," Lane replied, making an effort to switch her thoughts from her own troubles to Rowena's. "At least it'll make your aunt happy if you look into it. Speaking of Alice, did she leave any instructions for me?" Lane asked.

"She just said to sell everything you can to make some room before she gets back from Whitesburg with all those baskets. She can't imagine where she's going to put them."

Rowena tossed the message over her shoulder as she went out the door, and Lane noticed that her tone was as carefully flat and impersonal as it had been the previous afternoon at the musical. She looked after Rowena thoughtfully, trying to gauge the girl's feelings toward her. The new wary reserve seemed on its way to becoming permanent.

Disappointment and sadness shot through Lane. It'll work out, she thought, moving restlessly around the little shop. At least she hoped it would. She liked Rowena and she had been counting on the budding friendship between them.

Also, she didn't want Rowena gossiping to Janie and all her other friends about her, saying that she was stealing Thad away. Something like that could alienate half the community before her work really got underway.

She straightened some small wooden carvings on top of an old glass-topped counter and glanced longingly at the door. Oh, why had she told Alice she would come in and keep the shop open until six? The spring afternoon was more like June than late April; the very air tempted her to come outside. She could certainly use some time to wind down, too. Delcie had stretched her patience to the breaking point, and Rowena's hardening new attitude was bothering her a lot; it had been tugging at the back of her thoughts ever since the musical.

She thought about it for a few moments, idly running her fingers over the smooth lines of a wooden horse. Then, shaking her head, she shrugged helplessly and headed toward the tiny kitchen in the back of the store to make some tea. She was too tired to think of a solution right then; too tired of new people and of getting adjusted to them and worrying about what they thought of her. She needed some time to escape—from them and from her work—she decided; she really did need a day out under the tall pines just looking up into their branches and dreaming.

She put water into the kettle and turned on the ancient gas burner. While she waited for it to boil she walked over to the four-paned window and stared out. Even there in the middle of town everything was green, with trees growing down the hillsides to embrace the houses and shops in the valley. She could see five different kinds of trees from there. Vance had a lot of names to learn to add to his dogwood.

Vance! Her breath caught in her throat, and she leaned her forehead against the cool glass, the trees and hillside fading into the picture she'd been carrying around inside her head. The hard, strong lines of his face formed so clearly that they were almost real, and with them came the sparkling brown eyes that could change in a flash from mystery to laughter to desire.

His arms had been so incredibly strong around her. She still could feel the hardness of his broad chest against her breasts whenever she thought about him. Those few minutes by the dogwood tree had come back to her again and again; her body wouldn't let her forget the hot demand that had been in his lips and the desire that she'd seen in his eyes as he'd watched her go.

The teakettle began to whistle and she rushed to it just as the little bell on the door tinkled to announce a customer's arrival.

"Be with you in a minute," Lane called in the general direction of the shop. "Just go ahead and look around."

She went through the ritual of making the tea as

quickly as she could and left it to steep. She needed to go check on that customer; it seemed a little strange that whoever it was hadn't replied to her call.

She pushed aside the calico curtain that served as a door into the main part of the shop and stopped, the fabric clutched in her hand. There could be no mistaking the tall figure with his back to her; the bulk of his shoulders and the confident way he held them were indisputable. A strange feeling swept through her—a combination of excitement and fear. It was almost as if she had conjured him into being with the strength of her remembering. She felt surprise, but there was also a rightness to his being there.

"Vance," she breathed.

He turned, his dark eyes meeting hers, a smile in them and on his lips. Some of the wanting she'd last seen in them was still there, too, and as he walked toward her she lowered her gaze. An answering longing was flaring in her, and she didn't want him to see.

The Western-style work shirt he was wearing was pulled taut across his chest, and as he approached she could see the crisp black hairs curling in the vee where it was unbuttoned. His long legs were encased in tightly fitting faded jeans and his boots looked just as worn.

"I saw your jeep outside," he said in the husky tones that had been ringing in her memory. "It must be the only light green and white one in the county. What's that color called? Apple green?"

"I think so. I bought it because I loved the color; I didn't even look at any other combinations."

"Very sensible," he teased, his eyes holding hers, looking into them as if he wanted to read all the thoughts she'd had since they saw each other last.

Finally she turned away and gestured toward the private room behind her. "I've just made tea. Would you like some?"

"Sure. After a long day on the site I'll drink anything."

Lane flinched as the "site" flashed into her mind, but she didn't say anything. Somehow it felt so right for him to be there turning her dreamy mood into reality that she couldn't let anything unpleasant in to mar it.

She searched out two mugs and poured the tea while he explored the little room, ending up at the window where she had been.

"Sorry there's no fresh lemon," she said, joining him and handing him one of the mugs.

"That's OK." He took the steaming mug without looking at it. His eyes were on her face again, taking in every detail. Suddenly she was aware that her hair was mussed and windblown, barely staying in the loose knot she had made that morning low on the back of her head, and that her general appearance must show the long day of frustrating work she'd put in. She pushed at some of the escaping tendrils with one hand, then raised her tea to her lips.

"I don't know why I drink hot tea on a warm day like this. Maybe just because Alice doesn't have any ice here and I need my caffeine after the day I've had at Foggy Creek." All the exasperation Delcie had created flashed into her tone.

"Oh, what's this? Surely your noble natives haven't been giving you trouble!" he replied, his eyes dancing mischievously.

She tried to frown, but his tone was so light and his grin so infectious that she smiled back.

"Oh, just one, once in a while," she said, feeling the closeness that his charm seemed able to produce at will. How did he do it?

His attention was obviously not on her words, although he waited for her to go on. His eyes were caressing her face again, lingering on her lips.

When she stayed silent he said at last, "I've been wanting to see you again."

The words and the low tone struck a chord deep inside her; a matching thought was reverberating in her mind. She thrilled to the knowledge that he had felt the same way she had, but then she thought of how many times in the past few days she'd wanted the phone to ring and sudden anger stirred in her.

She looked straight at him, then sipped her tea. "I do have a telephone, you know."

"I've been out of town."

His eyes and the broadening of his smile told her that he'd read her feelings in her eyes, that he knew he had the power to make her angry and to make her wish he would call—the power to make her want him.

She dropped her gaze, trying to handle her conflicting emotions. How could he make her feel everything so strongly? She hardly knew him, but he had been on her mind for days, and now he was playing havoc with her feelings. One minute she was thrillingly happy and the next she was furious.

She tried to get back to neutral ground, carefully

keeping her voice even and pleasant. "I was just looking out this window before you came, thinking that there must be a half dozen different varieties of trees out there."

She didn't go on to tell him that she had had that thought in connection with him. However, as he looked down at her, his dark eyes burning in his tanned face, she knew with a certainty she couldn't explain that he had read her thoughts with uncanny accuracy.

"There must be," he repeated slowly, teasing her with his voice and with a grin. "And I only know the dogwood. Think you could give me more instruction in trees and other forms of wild life?"

The sparkle in his eyes drew her to him and took away her ability to answer as it began to erase her anger. He reached out to her and put his hand on the back of her neck with a confidence that said he was taking total control of her. He slid his long, bronzed fingers along her sensitive skin and into the heavy weight of her hair, destroying the remnants of her hairdo and, along with it, all her annoyance with him.

His hard fingers burned her skin and called up a welling desire from the deep center of her to flow along every inch of her body. They caressed her neck and the sensitive areas around her earlobes, tracing tiny paths of fire everywhere they touched. His eyes never left hers.

Finally he set his mug on the windowsill, then took hers from her and did the same with it, every languid movement heavy with purpose. The fear she'd felt on the mountain that first day and again at The Woodfern, the fear that she had no real power to resist him, flashed through her. Then his head bent to hers and every other emotion disappeared in a wave of wanting him.

His lips were as strong and sensual as her memories had told her, and his kiss took full possession of all her senses. At first she was very still, soaking in the touch of him, drinking in the salty, masculine taste and the piney, outdoor smell of him, just reveling in being so close to him again.

Then his tongue traced its way across the soft curves of her lips, demanding to come into the sweet recess of her mouth. She opened it to him and reached up to get her hands into his hair.

She pulled his head even closer to her, crushing their lips together as she let his probing tongue explore every corner of her mouth. Her fingers roamed through the thick silk of his hair, losing themselves in it at the same time as her senses became lost in the strength of the passion he had aroused.

His tongue came back to touch the tip of hers again, and she gasped a little; she couldn't let it go. Instinctively her lips closed around its honey, holding it so that she could touch it lightly with the tip of her own. The sweet, strong thrill of the contact surged into her breasts; her nipples hardened and reached out to him.

As if he knew that, he pulled her against him abruptly, almost roughly. She melted into him, her breasts pushing against the strength of his chest. She blended into the lean length of him and moved totally out of reality. There was no one in the world but the two of them, and they would have to stay this way forever; she didn't know how she'd ever existed by herself.

His hands began to roam over her back and her shoulders, to wander down her spine, each feathery touch a separate exploration, an individual riveting arousal that brought her even closer to him, that dissolved her into him. Then they began to trace her whole body, fanning out over the slim curves of her hips and moving up to caress the slim waist that they could almost span.

He pulled back from her a little bit then, just enough so that their bodies barely touched—her hard, throbbing nipples just grazing his chest. He moved against her slightly, then his magnetic hands continued their inexorable investigation up over her rib cage and on to the sides of her breasts. He cupped them hungrily, and she gasped with the thrill of it.

She pressed his head even closer to hers, and their kiss changed into a deep thrusting one that reached into the center of her being. She had never felt this way before in her entire life: so full of desire, so out of control. She was totally in his power; he could do anything with her.

With that thought fear flowed in and mingled with the excitement, and she tore her mouth from his and tried to pull away. She had to get her breath; she had to think; she had to achieve some semblance of sanity.

When she tried to escape, though, his arms held her even tighter. He crushed her to him and buried his face in her hair.

"This isn't really the reason I stopped by," he whispered. "But every time I see you I want to kiss you."

Their bodies still pressed together, he rocked her back and forth a little, and she relaxed, her thoughts fading again. She just luxuriated in the closeness she'd been wanting again since their lunch at The Woodfern. No, since they'd met that early morning on the mountain, she admitted to herself. Somehow she'd known since that first moment that the curves of her body would mold against his as if they were made to go together and that the warmth of his arms would be the most marvelous thing she'd ever known.

His low voice went on. "I was planning to save this until after the party."

His words hardly registered. Her senses were still so full of the touch and smell of him, the sweet sexiness of him, that she heard only the caressing tone of his voice and not what he was saying.

When she didn't speak he pulled away a little and tilted her chin up so that he could look at her. "I came by to ask you to a party. You'll come, won't you?"

At last her mind began to work again. "What party?" she asked huskily. "I haven't been invited to a party."

He chuckled. "You're being invited right now, silly. If you'll pay attention you'll find out all about it. Now listen. Saturday night. At my house. I'm giving a party for some legislators and other government officials and private businessmen. Everybody in this area who's interested in promoting tourism will be there. I want you to come."

Her brain began to function again. "But I'm not promoting tourism, remember? I'm opposed to it. How did I get on the guest list?"

"By being the most beautiful woman in East Kentucky," he answered. "I decided to make an exception in your case." His smile bathed her in light. "Will you come?"

"All right," she murmured. "What time?"

"Come at seven. There'll be drinks and dinner and dancing—a real East Kentucky shindig."

At that moment she couldn't have refused any request he would have made.

She looked up into his eyes, their depths shaded by lids heavy with desire. "I'll be there," she murmured.

His mouth was very near to hers, and she thought she would die if he didn't kiss her again.

She waited as his dark eyes caressed hers and then her lips, but when he moved back a little and dropped his gaze to her breasts, the tautness of her nipples clearly visible through the lace of her bra and the thin cotton of her shirt, she almost shuddered at the strength of her arousal. His eyes rested there for what seemed an eternity, and her blood burned in her veins. Then he let her go.

"I can't stay," he murmured. "If I touch you again . . ." His look, smoldering like black coal, finished the sentence without words.

"See you tomorrow," he whispered. And then he was gone.

Chapter Five

Lane surveyed her reflection in the long oak-framed mirror in the hall while Vance's housekeeper went to put away her bag and jacket. The music and laughing chatter drifting from the back of the house sounded as if the party were getting underway, and that excitement heightened the anticipation mixed with apprehension she'd been feeling all day.

She stepped back a little and turned on one high heel, trying to judge the effect of her tapered silk pants and full-sleeved blouse. Nervously she ran her hands into the thick hair at her temples, fluffing out the full curly style she'd chosen for the evening.

The hairstyle was one she didn't wear often, and the rich aquamarine color of her outfit reflected in her eyes to make them look unfamiliar, too. She hardly looked like herself.

Well, that was appropriate, she thought, giving

the girl in the mirror a wry smile. Every time she was with Vance she *was* a different person. He'd made her lose her head and behave like a wild thing every time she'd been with him. And now he'd taken possession of her thoughts as well. Since he'd left her in Alice's shop Monday afternoon she hadn't been able to get his look and his touch out of her mind.

She fiddled with the bow at her waist that fastened her wraparound top, wondering if she should loosen it. The vee of the neckline was low, the soft bright silk crossing at her breasts to show her creamy cleavage. A thrill shot through her as she thought of Vance's eyes on it, and she gave herself a reprimanding look.

During the few sane minutes she'd had since Monday she'd tried to concentrate on the dangers of getting involved with Vance, but she'd had little success. Her body kept overruling her mind and making the whole situation very simple: All she wanted was to see him again.

But tonight she had to remember the barriers between them, she thought distractedly. She had to remember that any relationship with him would have to overcome some tremendous differences.

She lifted one smooth brow ironically. So far this could hardly be called a relationship—it was more like an elemental reaction between two electrical charges. How could it be anything else when each time they met they were in each other's arms without warning, without talking and taking time to know each other?

She started to readjust the blouse, but at that moment the housekeeper came back to lead her through the house and out onto the enormous redwood deck. It sprawled around the back of the house on three levels, each with stairways leading downward through the trees and rocks to the edge of the lake.

Old-fashioned kerosene lamps and lanterns were everywhere, on the corners of the deck's railings and in the trees sitting on rocky ledges. Colorful quilts and hangings were draped over the railings, too, and handwoven baskets full of violets and trailing arbutus arranged amidst waxy dark green rhododendron leaves were on the tables and along the edges of the walkways. The entire effect was rustic and welcoming.

People were sitting and standing in groups, talking and laughing over the music of a bluegrass band. Lane glanced around quickly and her eyes found Vance; he was talking earnestly with two men in expensive business suits.

He was dressed in sleek-fitting black trousers and a Mexican wedding shirt made from the finest white cotton. Her breath caught—the contrast of the white against his dark good looks was stunning.

He saw her at the same instant, and almost immediately he was at her side, his hand strong and warm against the small of her back, his voice a caress to all her senses.

"How do you like it?"

"It's wonderful, Vance. It's a fantasy."

"You inspired it," he answered, his eyes bright with appreciation as he took in every detail of her appearance. "After our lunch at The Woodfern I asked around about local customs and I decided that the best kind of party would be an old-fashioned Appalachian Mountain pig roast."

Her heart leaped. He *had* been listening to her

that day! Her words had made more of an impression than she had thought; maybe those barriers were already coming down!

She smiled up at him warmly, and the answering glow in his eyes made her eyes wander to his lips. With an effort she turned to look toward the lake.

"So that's why the circle of lanterns down by the lake," she said. "That's the barbecue pit."

"Right. One pig roasted plain, and one pig and half a steer barbecued, I believe Mrs. Howard said. She made all the arrangements."

"Vance." A booming voice said the name as if it were an announcement of the highest importance. They turned to see a tall, silver-haired man coming through the double doors of the house, his hand extended in greeting.

"So good to see you again," he went on.

"It's good to see you," Vance replied. "Senator Cravens, this is Lane Matthews."

"Nice to meet you," the man announced in the same serious tone. "I always like to meet a pretty lady." He took her hand and looked into her eyes, but his own were empty of expression, and immediately he turned back to Vance, all business.

"I want to tell you that you're the greatest thing that's happened to tourism in Kentucky since interstate highways," he pronounced. "Greenbriar is going to give a tremendous boost to the economy around here. . . ."

Lane stopped listening. She didn't want to think about Vance as the greatest thing for tourism; she didn't want to think about Greenbriar or any of the other problems between them.

All she wanted now was to forget why he was in Kentucky and in her life in the first place, to stand very still and marvel at how right it felt to be in the warm circle of his arm. Her senses were coming alive in the warm, dusky evening, as they did only when she was with him, and she didn't want anything to spoil that marvelous feeling.

She looked around her, drinking in her surroundings as Vance continued to listen to the senator. He had drawn her very close, as if to let her know that she was included even though she wasn't participating in the conversation, and his strong arm around her and the touch of his lean thigh against hers seemed to say that his real attention was on her.

The fragrances of the flowers that surrounded them drifted to her and brought the mountains very close, even though the wooded ridges were almost invisible in the deepening dusk. The colors of the blossoms seemed to Lane to be growing stronger as the light began to fade; the white and pink of the trailing arbutus almost glowed in the smoky half-light.

The music wasn't loud, but its minor, bluegrass tones floated on to the deck and out toward the lake, and the lively beat made her want to dance, to float with it. She began to wait for just one thing: for the senator to stop talking, to give Vance back to her so that he could take her in his arms and dance with her, so that she could feel the warmth of his masculine length against her once more.

"Well, hello there." The senator's booming words intruded into Lane's thoughts and for a second she thought he was talking to her. He wasn't. A striking brunette was joining them, her sleek red dress a flame in the darkening evening.

"Gloria," Vance said. "Meet Lane Matthews

and Senator Cravens. Gloria Sullivan is my advertising consultant from New York."

A slight coolness filtered into the warm glow Lane had been feeling. Vance's advertising consultant? The woman was so beautiful, so sleekly confident. Was she *only* a business associate to Vance?

The senator welcomed Gloria into the group by directing his next remarks to her. "I was just telling Vance that he fits right in," he blared, clapping Vance on the back as if he were welcoming him into a circle of good old boys. "He surely knows how to give a party. Why, I haven't been to an old-fashioned pig roast since my first campaign for the Senate ten years ago." His hearty laugh rang out. "Looks like it takes a guy from Chicago to come down here and remind us of our roots—make us all feel at home."

A second breath of coolness touched Lane, this one stronger, strong enough to make her hand tremble as she played with the bow at her waist. How could she have been so naive?

Vance hadn't remembered what she'd told him about the mountain culture so that he could enrich his life as she had hoped! He hadn't planned this party with its mountain theme to please her—he was using what he'd learned from her to further his hateful project!

A waiter came by with a tray of drinks, and Lane took a glass, totally unaware of its contents. She'd been absolutely right to be afraid of a deeper involvement with him. In spite of the closeness they'd felt before, in spite of the rightness she'd felt at being by his side, they were as far apart as ever.

The senator launched into another lecture, and

Lane looked around the deck and the grounds, trying to find a familiar face among the guests. She wanted to escape, to get away from Vance and try to straighten out the havoc inside her—to reconcile the war between the electric warmth of being so near to him physically and the terrifying cold of being so far from him in other ways. No matter how magnetic the attraction was that pulled their bodies together every time they met, there was a terrible gulf between them, and she'd better recognize it now.

She saw no one she knew, however, and before she could think of another simple way to leave the group she found herself between Gloria and the senator in the buffet line. They filled their plates from the platters of succulent meats that the waiters had brought up from the roasting pit and with the shucky beans, potato salad, dried apples and cornbread that were traditional mountain fare. There were also a wide selection of fruits that Vance had had brought in and several enormous leafy green salads.

Lane mechanically put a small serving of each dish on her plate and, hardly aware of what she was doing, followed Gloria to one of the many small tables scattered around the deck. When the four of them were settled the senator and Vance continued to talk business, and Gloria turned the full force of her energetic attention on Lane.

"Vance tells me that you're researching old folkways or the sociology of the mountains or something like that," she said brightly. "He said he got the idea for the theme of this party from you."

Lane nodded, trying to concentrate on the conversation instead of on Vance. "I suppose he did."

"Well, it was certainly a good one." Gloria smiled at her warmly. "Everything is just fascinating." She gestured toward the quilts and the basket centerpieces. "I can't believe all the things these people can do."

The condescension in Gloria's tone was so irritating that Lane bristled. "What people do you mean?"

"Why these . . . mountaineers. Or hill people, I guess you'd call them." She smiled in her slightly superior way. "I'm not really current on the terminology, but I suppose it isn't acceptable to use the term 'hillbilly.'"

"Only if you're one of them," Lane answered dryly. "I wouldn't, if I were you."

"Well, I won't. I certainly don't want to start some sort of a feud," Gloria said, laughing. She took a sip of wine. "You'll have to give me lessons on how to behave," she went on, her tone implying that they were sharing a secret. "I'll be back soon to spend some time here."

That news made Lane's stomach contract, but she reminded herself swiftly that it was none of her business; she had no hold on Vance, whatever his relationship with Gloria might be.

"You might try behaving as you would in New York or anyplace else," she answered. "We *are* all members of the human race."

Gloria smiled tightly at the rebuke. "How true!" she said, her tone traced with sarcasm. "And how wise! You really should be in philosophy instead of sociology, Lane."

She took another sip of wine, then turned back to Lane, her manner suddenly brisk. It was as if they had had a little skirmish to point out their differences, and now that it was out of the way they could get down to business.

"I'd like you to introduce me to some of your resource people," the woman stated confidently, as if all she had to do was to mention the idea and it was done. "You must know some real characters who would be just great in an advertisement."

The senator was finally concentrating on his food instead of on the sound of his own voice, and Vance overheard Gloria's request. He turned to look at Lane, his dark eyes compelling, his smile full of confidence and charm. "That's a good idea," he said. "Why don't you do that?"

His voice was low and smooth, and his eyes were warm, but Lane felt as if all the warmth had suddenly gone out of the air. How could he ask such a thing when he knew how she felt about the ad campaign—about his whole horrendous project? How could he care so little about her feelings?

The hurt stabbed at her, but she tried to hide it. She kept her voice level, neutral, as she answered, "Oh, I don't know. Most of my contacts are pretty new, because I've only been here a short while myself; I need to get to know them better before I bring strangers along."

"That's OK," Gloria said brightly. "It'll be a couple of weeks or so before I get back. I just dropped in today to see Vance on my way home from a business trip to Dallas."

Lane concentrated on cutting a piece of the pork tenderloin on her plate, but when she put it into her mouth the delicacy tasted like sand. If Gloria had just dropped by to see Vance socially, then their relationship *wasn't* all business.

"I'd really appreciate any help you can give us,

Lane," Vance persisted. "Gloria needs to get a feel for the area and, as you pointed out to me, that's hard to do when you're coming in cold."

Lane stared into his suave dark eyes, her own burning with anger. Why was he pushing this? Was he so wrapped up in his business that he didn't even realize how she felt?

And now he and Gloria were "us." What a fool she had been! She'd let him kiss her and turn her into mush every time she saw him, and he had probably just been using her for a substitute until Gloria could get there!

"I don't see how I can give you any help," she said stiffly. "As far as I can tell we aren't working on the same project, nor are we aiming for the same goals."

He raised one eyebrow. "Aren't we?" he teased, his eyes glinting intimately. "Don't we have at least one of the same goals?"

She felt heat rush into her cheeks at the insinuation in his words and his tone, and she looked down at her plate so that he couldn't see the fury and embarrassment in her face.

At last she looked at him again. "No, we aren't, Vance. We have no goals at all in common."

"Then I must have misunderstood," he replied calmly. "We need to talk about this."

Damn him! How could he sit there totally unruffled, completely unmoved, and say those bland, meaningless words to her? How could he want to talk when she wanted nothing so much as to toss the contents of her wineglass straight into his handsome, composed face?

The fact that she didn't respond to him and the tension that was radiating from her caused a brief, uncomfortable silence to fall over the table. Then the senator eased it by directing a remark to Gloria, and Lane began to pick at her food, trying to act as if Vance no longer existed.

As soon as dinner was over Senator Cravens led Gloria away to dance with him, and Lane turned to Vance. "Thank you for inviting me," she said formally. "I have to go now."

"You aren't going anywhere until I find out why you're suddenly treating me as if I have two heads," he said firmly. "We're going to talk."

"We are *not!*" she countered. "I never want to speak to you again!"

"Well, you will," he answered, gritting the words through his teeth. He took a firm hold on her upper arm and began walking, holding her very near him. He smiled and spoke briefly to several people as they made their way around the groups of guests, but he didn't say anything else to Lane as they descended the steps of the deck and then the narrow path that led to the shore of the lake.

He led her past the fire, its embers still glowing, then along the narrow, rocky beach and around a tall outcropping of rock. Fury surged in Lane, but the thrill of being so near to him again was mixed with it. The electric current that always flowed between them was entering her through his long fingers, and she couldn't bring herself to jerk away from him.

Finally he stopped and turned her to face him. "Now explain," he demanded. "Why are you acting this way?"

"The fact that you don't already know just proves that it would be useless to try to tell you," she snapped. "I tried to explain something to you at The Woodfern, but you evidently didn't understand a word of what I said."

"Let me tell you what I understood at The Woodfern," he said, his voice suddenly very soft. He had stopped so that she was standing with her back to the big rock, almost touching it, and now he put one hand on it, leaning very near to her.

"Let me tell you what I understood at The Woodfern," he repeated, "and at Alice's shop Monday." He reached out to touch the side of her face as he had done that first day on the mountain, and one hard finger traced a shimmering path around her ear in rhythm with his mesmerizing tones.

"Vance, leave me alone," she said, pulling away, trying desperately to hold on to her anger, to use it to bolster the realization that she had to stop letting him touch her and melt her into insensibility every time they met.

The rock left her no place to turn, but she wouldn't have gone even if she could have; his hand was caressing her neck and her treacherous body was already crying out for more.

"I understood that we need each other," he went on as if she hadn't spoken, moving even closer to her.

Tremors raced up and down her body as it yearned to touch his. Now she couldn't remember why she didn't want him to touch her; she could think of nothing except the way his leanly muscled length had felt against her the day in the shop. The masculine scent of him was filling her senses, and desire began draining away her ability to think, and with it her resistance.

"I understood that you want me as much as I

want you, and that this is what we should be doing instead of looking daggers at each other across the table," he murmured.

He placed both hands against the rock and bent to kiss her then, his lips already on fire when they touched hers.

She didn't even try to resist the urgency of his mouth. She met it with an eagerness of her own, an eagerness born of the longing that had been her constant companion since he had left her Monday with the imprint of his lips on her mouth and desire throbbing in her as it never had before.

As his lips took hers, his tongue moved into her mouth as if it belonged there, touching and exploring, caressing, expertly sending fuel to the fire that was beginning to burn in her. She moved gladly into that sphere where his touch always took her—a place that held nothing and no one but the two of them and the pulsing, urgent need that their bodies had for each other.

All she wanted was to make the moment last, to intensify it, to be even closer to him, but before she could move to bring him nearer his lips were suddenly gone from hers. He pulled away and stood looking down at her, still caressing her, but without touching her now. His eyes devoured first her face and then her breasts, their depths glowing with pleasure and passion.

"Ah, but you're beautiful," he said, his voice low and husky. "You're a beautiful woman, Lane."

He reached out to her slowly then, as if he had been waiting years for this moment to come. His strong hands carefully traced the shape of one and then the other of her trembling breasts, his eyes following every movement of his fingers, their dark fire stroking her and fueling the flame in her as forcefully as his fingers did.

Her nipples thrilled to him, hardening, straining toward him. Her breath caught with her need to feel his hands on them, and his eyes moved back to hers, smiling, tantalizing.

Then, deliberately, surely, he cupped her soft breasts in his big hands and took their yearning tips between his thumbs and fingers, fondling and teasing them until flames of wanting leaped in her and she thought she could no longer bear it.

"Oh, Lane, Lane . . ." He sighed raggedly, then his hands left her breasts, and he pulled her to him, pressing her against his own need as if only she could answer it.

His lips moved over her hair, her face, and searched for her mouth once more. They took hers urgently, surely, as if there were an understanding between them now, a communication that had passed between them without any words. Now they clung to each other as if this closeness had been theirs for years, as if this confident touching and melding of their lips, their tongues and their bodies were rooted deep in the past.

The riotous passion that she had for him was building in her again just as it had done before, but she was no longer afraid of it. Suddenly it was a natural part of her, a part that had been there all along, just waiting for Vance to come.

A sound intruded, floating into the moonlit retreat on the mild breeze that had sprung up with the loss of the light. It forced its way into Lane's consciousness, and she recognized a voice, the all-too-familiar voice that had dominated her evening. It broke the spell.

"Damn!" Vance muttered, taking his lips from hers. "How did he find us?"

In a moment they became aware that Senator Cravens hadn't found them at all; he was above them on a rocky ledge that extended over the narrow beach. He wasn't talking to them; he was earnestly holding forth to a companion, but the intimacy that had surrounded them was gone.

"You won't find a prettier view anywhere. . . ." The words came down to them clearly, bringing the outside world in and Lane back to her senses. Suddenly the moonlight reflecting off the lake, the scent of the pines that covered the hillside, even the man in her arms, belonged not just to her, but to everyone.

The doubts that had plagued her all evening filtered in again, and her mind began to function. She pulled away from Vance as quickly as she had gone to him. She had to get away and think, to try to decide whether she could trust him.

"We'd better get back to the party," she said breathlessly. "You don't want to be rude and leave your guests for too long."

"I haven't," he answered, reaching to pull her to him again. "Lane, I want to talk to you."

She moved away from him and ran her hands through the thick blond hair at her temples, shaking her head as if that would clear up the confusing thoughts it held.

"Not now, Vance," she said and turned to lead the way back up the winding path. She couldn't talk to him now, she couldn't be with him any more tonight. She had to get away from that electrifying force that emanated from him, had to try to find her control and her old self again, the self that had existed before she met him.

He followed her, and as they emerged from the tree-lined rocky path on to the first level of the redwood deck they came face to face with Senator Cravens and Gloria.

"Vance!" Gloria said enthusiastically. "I was wondering where you were." Carefully she included Lane in her smile. "The senator has just been telling me all about Kentucky, and it sounds just fascinating. I can't wait to explore the hills and meet some people."

The senator rumbled something about making a real Kentuckian out of Gloria, but she spoke again quickly before he could start a new monologue.

"It'll be so much fun to go exploring with you when I come back next month," she said happily to Lane. "I just can't wait."

Lane was still caught up in the jumble of feelings that Vance's hands and lips had created in her, and in her determination to get away and try to sort them out, so Gloria's remark hardly registered.

When she didn't answer Vance said encouragingly, "You *are* going to take Gloria to meet some of your contact people, aren't you, Lane? Later, when you've had time to establish some rapport with them?"

Suddenly the words made sense and the reality of the party faded away again. But this time, instead of moving from it into a warm, dark cocoon with Vance, Lane found herself all alone in a cold prism of light. The deck beneath her feet was no longer solid, dependable wood—it was made of the most delicate, treacherous glass.

Was this the reason Vance had insisted on their going down to the lake to "talk"? Was this the reason he had been holding her close and kissing her, caressing her breasts and driving her mad with desire? Had he been planning all along to soften her up, then ask her again to help Gloria with his advertising campaign?

Her horrified mind took the idea a step further. Was that the reason he'd asked her to the party in the first place? The reason he'd taken her in his arms at Alice's shop and then left her there feeling that she could no longer live without his touch?

Disappointment washed over her, then anger followed, rushing through every vein in her body, stiffening her stance and her determination to learn to resist him. She ignored Gloria and her question, turning to Vance as if they were alone.

"I'm sorry you misunderstood me at The Woodfern," she told him, every word a separate cube of ice. "I didn't mean to encourage . . ." She looked around, sweeping her eyes over the festive scene, the charming handicrafts, the band, the flickering lanterns, the groups of guests earnestly talking business. She looked at Gloria and the senator, then back at Vance. ". . . tourism," she finished sarcastically.

He looked puzzled; a frown came onto his handsomely chiseled face, and he reached out questioningly to her as if to take her arm.

Quickly she stepped back and turned to address all three of them. "I really do have to go now," she said. "Good night." She walked away, the high heels of her sandals clicking against the redwood deck.

He followed beside her in a second. "Lane, if

you can't stay, at least wait until I can walk you to the door."

"Never mind," she snapped, meeting the warmth in his eyes with the bleak coldness in her own. "I told you, I didn't want to encourage anything."

He stopped, standing totally still, his eyes going as hard as hers, their color changing from deep brown to ebony. The animosity crackling from her every pore was as strong as her desire for him had been a few moments earlier, and it reacted with the determination in him to form a bond that was just as inescapable as their passion had been.

His eyes stared into hers, and when he spoke it was with a surety that told her volumes about the power he was accustomed to wielding. "I'm not easily discouraged, Lane."

She turned and left him, but as she collected her things and stepped out again into the fragrant night, she realized that, hard as she'd tried, she hadn't even been able to walk out on him. He had let her go—for the moment.

Chapter Six

*E*ven the long drive back to Covey on the dark, winding roads didn't calm her, and by the time she got home she was restlessly wondering how she could ever get through the long evening and the night that stretched ahead. She parked the jeep in Alice's side yard and hurried into the house, wishing desperately for someone to talk to.

She didn't want to discuss the party or Vance—she wanted someone to distract her because she was determined not to think about the evening at all. It was too confusing and too infuriating to realize that she could have let her impetuous body blind her to Vance's real motives. And it hurt too much to remember his mouth and his hands on her.

When he called she'd somehow manage to break this new bond that was between them. His determination to have his way couldn't be as strong as that animal attraction had been between them, and *that* was gone forever, destroyed by his dishonesty. She'd never let him touch her again.

She went up the back stairs and changed quickly into jeans and a shirt. If she couldn't find Alice or Rowena she would take a long walk. A climb in the moonlit hills should calm her down; in fact, it sounded wonderful after all the tension of the evening.

She started down the wide front stairs, and as soon as her clogs sounded on the wooden steps, Alice called out from the big kitchen-keeping room, "Rowena, is that you?"

"No, Alice," Lane responded. "I'm home early."

Alice appeared in the hall doorway. "Oh, I was hoping it was Rowena," she said. For a split second she looked past Lane at an invisible spot on the wall; then, with a ragged sigh, she met Lane's eyes. Alice's face was blotchy, and her eyes were puffy and red from crying.

A rush of sympathy twisted in Lane. Alice was standing slumped against the wide facing of the door, stooped, suddenly years older than she had been that morning.

"Alice, what's wrong?"

The concern in Lane's tone brought a welling of tears, but Alice swallowed hard and with a visible effort kept them from falling. "It's a long story. . . ." she began, then the tears threatened again. She shook her head and gestured for Lane to follow her back into the big, cheerful room. She waved Lane to a seat at the scarred table, then busied herself with the teakettle, which was just beginning to whistle.

When she had poured the water and moved the kettle off the heat, she began to talk.

"We had an argument a while ago, and Rowena rushed out the door, mad as a wet hen," she said, bringing quilted calico placemats and two hand-thrown mugs to the table. "She didn't say a word about where she was going or when she'd be back. I'm just thankful she didn't take the car, or she'd have a wreck as sure as I'm sitting here."

She slumped into the chair across from Lane to wait for the tea to steep, pure misery in her eyes. "One of these days she'll really go away, Lane. She won't listen to me anymore. I'm going to lose that girl."

Lane reached across to touch her hand. "Now, Alice, you don't know that. Maybe she just needs to take a little vacation as soon as school is out."

"No, it's more than that; she's too unhappy," Alice said. "She'll never stay in Covey unless . . . oh, unless she married somebody here. Rowena's restless; she's looking for something."

Alice went to get the teapot, and Lane watched her. Her carriage was ramrod straight, as stiff as the white starched curtains at the black-paned windows.

As Alice poured the tea Lane built up her courage to broach the difficult subject, and finally she said, "Alice, I think Rowena's problem is very simple. I think she's in love with Thad."

Alice's hand shook, and she set the teapot back onto the trivet with a thump. Her eyes flashed to Lane's and then away, her face falling into an uncompromising mask.

"She may think she is, but she's not," she

snapped. "She's built that up in her mind all this time just to be contrary."

"I don't think so," Lane answered. "I've seen her look at him, Alice. . . ."

The slam of the front door interrupted her, and almost immediately Rowena was framed in the doorway. Her loose red hair was windblown, and the tension in the way she stood suggested that she might fly off into the night again at any moment.

She glanced briefly at her aunt without speaking, then turned a passionate, direct gaze on Lane. "Did Alice tell you about your phone call?" she asked, her voice as highly charged as her body. "Someone called you while you were at the big party up on Jackson Lake."

Her tone was challenging, as if she would have loved to draw Lane into a gigantic argument. The withdrawn look she'd had the day before had been replaced by one of angry hurt.

Disappointment washed over Lane. Well, forget the little sister bit, she told herself. We'll be lucky just to keep this whole relationship civil for the rest of the time that I'll be here.

"I suppose it must have been Thad," she responded, keeping her voice as level as she could.

"That's right," Rowena shot back. "I thought you said you went with him to Junior's place just because he was helping you with your work." Her tone was filled with nasty sarcasm as she went on accusingly, "Well, tonight he called you for a date."

Alice broke into the spate of words. "Now, Rowena, you don't know what he wanted. . . ."

"No, he didn't talk to me long enough to say, and he certainly didn't leave a message."

Alice spoke again. "Rowena, get hold of your-self. It's none of your business who calls Lane, nor why. Thad Campbell is nothing to you."

The words stung, and Rowena turned her blaz-ing eyes from Lane to her aunt. "Well, he could be—if you two would stay out of it. You won't ever let me spend one second talking to him, and Lane's always around, making up to him."

"Rowena, that's not fair—" Lane started to protest, but Alice cut her off.

She stood up, her chair scraping the floor. "You remember your manners, girl," she lashed out. "Lane is company in our house and a visitor in the mountains. Don't you go insulting her."

"She's not company, she's a boarder," Rowena shot back, as if Lane weren't there, "and I don't know why she had to come to the mountains in the first place."

Alice's face flushed red with embarrassment at her niece's rudeness. She flashed a swift, apologet-ic glance at Lane, then concentrated on Rowena, holding the girl stock-still in her steely gaze. Her voice crackled with feelings—anger, determination and something else as well, something that sound-ed to Lane almost like fear. "You are to forget Thad Campbell, do you hear me? He's no good; he never has been and he never will be. He's nothing but trouble and he'll have nothing to do with any kin of mine."

Rowena's mouth opened to protest, but Alice's voice marched on. "I do not want to hear his name mentioned in this house again, and I forbid you to so much as to speak to him."

Rowena's face went chalky under the outdoor

rosiness that had been in her cheeks. She stared back at her aunt, but she didn't say a word.

Alice went on inexorably. "Now that that's settled, you apologize to Lane and go to your room." Her tone softened. "Get some rest and everything will look different in the morning."

She continued to hold Rowena's gaze and finally the girl grudgingly turned to Lane. "I'm sorry," she muttered insincerely. Then she was gone, her feet clattering on the stairs.

Alice sat down heavily. Her eyes were full of tears again. "I know I'll lose her now," she murmured. "She's too old to be handled like that, but I just lost my head." She twisted the cup around on the soft mat, staring into it as if it held the answers she needed.

"I'm scared," she admitted softly. She looked up and repeated the words in a stronger voice. "I'm scared, Lane. I don't want her to go away, but I'm afraid of what'll happen if she stays here."

"Alice, maybe it isn't quite so bleak as you think," Lane said, trying to comfort her. "Thad seems to be a decent guy and if he *were* interested in Rowena . . ."

The hurting brown eyes went hard, and Alice looked right through Lane. "Over my dead body," she said flatly. She rose swiftly, restlessly, as if she couldn't stand to think about it. "I've got to get some air," she muttered and, taking a shawl from the pegged rack by the door, she went out across the back porch.

Lane rinsed out the teacups, put out the kitchen lights and climbed the stairs to her room, sadness settling over her and dampening the restlessness that had filled her earlier. There'd be no warm, happy home in Covey during the time she was there, and there'd be no warm, happy relationship with Vance Morgan, either. She was as alone as she had always been.

Rowena's words rang in her mind, and as she went into her little room and crossed to the window to stare out into the blackness she, too, wondered why she had ever come to the mountains in the first place.

Lane breathed a sigh of relief when she and Thad finally reached the mouth of the hollow and turned out onto the narrow blacktop highway. The rocky track that led up Bittercreek to the houses of Old Man Charlie and his relatives was one of the roughest she'd encountered, and steering the jeep around its ruts and stones had added several twists to the knot of muscles at the back of her neck. She reached up with one hand to try to rub it away, holding on to the steering wheel with the other.

"Here, better let me do that," Thad said easily, his big hand brushing hers away, his long fingers massaging out the tension. "If you don't keep both hands on the wheel you're liable to have us in the ditch again the way you did over on Nearcat Ridge."

They both laughed at the memory of their adventure earlier in the week, and as she met his smiling eyes Lane thought how nice it would be if his touch could stir the same fire in her that Vance's did.

She and Thad were beginning to build a friendship; they had visited several other people in addition to his grandfather in the two weeks since the night of Vance's party, and they had talked for hours as they'd driven along the winding roads. Thad loved to explore the old buildings and listen to the old people, and he delighted in sharing the customs and music and stories of his native mountains with Lane. He was fun to be with, and they had so many things in common, she thought. Many things, but not that irresistible magnetism that drew her body to Vance's like a blossom to the sun. Hurt twisted in her again, and she forced her mind away from it.

"I'll do my best to stay on the road," she promised. "I certainly don't want to keep you away from your shop while we push this thing out of a ditch. I already feel guilty enough for taking up your whole morning."

"It's been a pleasure, Lane," he said, his musical voice low. She glanced at him again. There were the admiration and interest that she'd seen before in his eyes, but the friendly, wry expression on his face told her that he knew theirs was a comradeship and nothing more.

He's so sensitive, she thought. How can Alice be so set against him? What can he possibly have done to make her say he'd date Rowena over her dead body?

"Thad . . ." she began, but then she didn't know what she wanted to say. She couldn't very well ask him why Alice disapproved of him, or whether he was interested in Rowena. So instead she mentioned the pictures they'd just taken of Charlie's cabin and of Charlie himself. They chatted about inconsequential things until she pulled the jeep up in front of his shop.

"Want to come over to the café for some lunch?" she asked, hating to lose the warmth of his company. "Are you hungry?"

"No, not yet," he answered. "And I really need to get to work. I've owed a dulcimer to a customer from Ohio for over two months now. If I don't ship it pretty soon he'll be back down here to get his money."

She smiled her understanding and, with a regretful wave, she left him. Thad's friendly, energetic presence had been the only comfort she'd had during the past couple of weeks, and each time they'd parted she had resisted stepping back into her loneliness.

It seemed that ever since that exhausting night of Vance's party, the life she'd begun to build for herself in Covey had slowly been unraveling. Alice had been too preoccupied and withdrawn to confide in her again, and Lane hadn't felt free to take up the older woman's time with her own problems, not that she would have been able to talk about Vance in any case. She had made a point of letting Rowena know that Thad had called her to make plans to take her to see Charlie instead of for a date, and since then Rowena had been civil to her, but she hadn't shown the earlier friendliness she'd had for Lane. And the other part of her personal life that had begun in Covey—Vance—had suddenly become nonexistent.

Savagely she pushed in on the clutch of the jeep as she downshifted for the steepness of the hill. Evidently, in spite of what he'd said when she left him, he *was* easy to discourage, she thought. She had planned, all through that long, horrible night and the days that had followed, to tell him when he called that she didn't want to see him again, and she'd assured herself that eventually she would forget how she'd felt in his arms. However, she needn't have bothered to plan—the telephone had remained stubbornly silent.

She fought down the riot of emotions that rose in her every time she thought of him and turned the jeep into a parking place in front of the small, homey café that everyone called Mattie's. She wasn't hungry, either, but she didn't want to be alone with her thoughts. She wanted to sit in the cheerful room and be surrounded by the familiar banter and daily routine of Covey's unofficial community center while she made some notes about Old Man's cabin and his explanation of how to notch a log.

And while she tried to pull her mind away from Vance, she admitted as she took her bag and got out of the jeep. It would always be a mystery to her how she could have hurt so much these past few days over losing someone she'd never had, someone who had made a complete fool of her. She had asked herself a thousand times how she could have felt so at home in his arms when he'd had no feeling for her at all.

Mattie led her to the last empty booth and took her order for iced tea and chicken salad. While she waited she rummaged in her bag for her camera, took out the film she'd used that morning, packaged it for mailing and replaced it with a fresh roll. Then she took out her notebook and rapidly began filling it with her neat, round script. She'd learned that keeping busy was a marvelous antidote for thinking.

Halfway down the first page she became aware

that someone was standing beside her. "Just set it down over there, please, Mattie," she murmured without looking up. "I'll finish this before I eat."

"I'm sorry I didn't bring your food," a deep voice answered. "I only brought myself. Is it all right if I set *me* down over here until you're finished?"

Wild, unreasoning elation leaped in her at the sound, and she looked up into Vance's dark eyes. She drank in his chiseled features and the curve of his sensual lips as he smiled at her. His tan was deeper than ever; he must have been spending a lot of time outdoors at Greenbriar.

Silently she nodded. He slid into the booth, his long legs touching hers in the process, and the electricity that had been there from the first flashed between them again. Even without feeling his skin against hers she remembered his touch, and her body tingled with wanting it.

She pushed away the feeling and sat back in her own side of the booth. Her eyes were fastened on him—his sleek, dark head bent over the menu Mattie brought him; his lean, strong fingers, which she knew could create magic, holding it with the casual confidence that marked his every move.

Anger began to build in her. She had meant no more to him than that piece of paper in his hand. He had held her in that same easy way, and with no more feeling. She had been on fire for him; she had felt a mysterious closeness to him, an instinctive communication on some deep, elemental level—when all the time he had been thinking only of his business.

Mattie returned with more iced water and waited while he considered the menu, as if the decision he was about to make was one of the most important of his life. Fury seethed in Lane, and she almost blurted out that he shouldn't bother to order, that she wasn't going to sit there and have lunch with him, that she was never going to spend any time with him again.

She opened her mouth, the words about to tumble out, and then thought of how ridiculous that would sound. After all, they had never formally dated; they had no relationship at all. He had simply asked her to one party, a party to which half the state had been invited.

But she had to, she thought, staring at her hands as she restlessly rearranged the silverware that had been wrapped in her napkin. Somehow she had to make him go away. That same electric current was in the air, the one that would tell her of his presence even if she were blind and deaf. That magnetism was there, drawing her to him, and if she let it, it would destroy her.

After he had ordered and Mattie had left, he smiled at Lane, his even teeth flashing. "Do you have some interesting plans for the afternoon?" he asked casually. His voice was pleasant, as if they had just had a brief interruption in an ordinary conversation.

She stared at him for a long minute, his words and his tone fueling her resentment. Finally she spoke. "And why would you possibly care what plans I have?" she demanded sarcastically, her fury almost choking her. "Do you want me to drop them and help organize your advertising campaign?"

"No, I want to be included in them," he answered, calmly taking a drink of his water. "I'm just trying to accept an invitation that you offered me a few weeks ago; this has nothing to do with my business."

"Well, I've learned something during the weeks since I gave you that invitation," she replied shortly. "I've found out that *everything* you're involved in has something to do with your business."

Her voice was tight and unsteady; it held all the hurt and resentment that had grown in her for the past few days, and the accusation that he couldn't be trusted burned in her eyes.

His dark eyes searched her face. "What are you talking about?" he demanded, his voice rough.

"I'm talking about the fact that the only thing in the whole world that matters to you is your business!" she shot back.

She had meant to stop there, but the sense of betrayal that she had lived with for the past few days rose in a wave of hurtful words that had to come out.

"I'm talking about the fact I won't be in your arms again with my own feelings raw and vulnerable to you and yours miles away wrapped up in your precious advertising campaign and Greenbriar," she declared passionately, leaning toward him across the little table. "So if all you want from me are 'characters' for Gloria, then forget it. You can find them yourself."

He reached across to take her hand, and fire shot through her. "You're wrong, Lane," he said, his voice low. "You're all wrong about me."

"No, I'm not," she replied, moving her hand away from the galvanizing touch of his fingers. "And now that I know that I won't let you make a fool of me again."

The intensity that came into his eyes was born of an anger that was just beginning, but there was something else there, too. There was a dark hurt hovering behind the light, a vulnerability that seemed very foreign to him.

"You can't sit there and tell me what my feelings are and what's important to me," he said flatly. "And I would never make a fool of you."

She bit her lip to keep back the tears that were pushing at her eyelids and stared down at her glass. She was moving it around in little circles, leaving rings of moisture on the white Formica. She felt as if she, too, were going around in circles, whirled by the force of the contradictory emotions that filled her.

"This big realization of yours is a farce," he said simply, his voice hard with anger. "I've given you no reason to mistrust me."

"You certainly have!" she retorted. "All you ever wanted from me was help with Greenbriar."

"That isn't true," he said firmly. "And don't put 'want' in the past tense—I still want something from you."

She glanced up at him quickly, ready to defend herself, to deny his request. His anger was gone, though, and there was an openness in his face and in his voice, an honesty that paralleled her own.

He watched her closely, as if a great deal depended on his convincing her to listen to him. "I want to be with you," he said simply, "and I want to learn what you've been trying to tell me."

Silence lay between them. Her heart was suddenly beating with a wild, thudding rhythm, and though the cheerful noises of voices and dishes that she had wanted when she came into the café swirled around her, they seemed very far away. He was creating a private world for them again, and in spite of her anger with him and disgust for her own weakness, she was longing to follow him into it, just as she always did.

"Won't you take me with you to see the mountains your way?" he went on, pushing for an answer as if he sensed her weakening.

She took a sip of water, her mind rushing frantically to make a decision, to find the resolution not to see him again that she had nurtured so carefully during these past bleak days.

How could she drive the isolated roads and climb into the hollows and hills with him as she had with Thad and not end up floating in his arms again, throbbing with desire? And how could she make love with him and not be lost forever?

But how could she not take this opportunity to try to change his perspective? Wasn't that the only hope to minimize the damage Greenbriar would do? Didn't she owe that to the mountains and the people she loved? This was the chance she'd been begging for, and she had to take it. It was too important to her work, and her work was all she would have when the summer was over.

She would have to tell him yes, she thought, but they couldn't continue as they had done. She couldn't just step right back into the intimate world he was creating without some order, some protection. There had to be some rules.

She sat up very straight. "All right," she said. "I'll show you what I see in Appalachia." She held his gaze with an intensity that radiated the hurt she'd been living with. "But this will have to be strictly a professional relationship, Vance. I have a job to do and I just can't handle anything else right now."

She wouldn't go into the arms of a stranger again, she thought, and today she had realized that she didn't know Vance Morgan at all.

And she would *never* know him, she decided, as the next few weeks went by and their relationship fell into a pattern. Once or twice a week, sometimes more often, he swung into the jeep beside her, and they went to see the new friends she had made. They drove the narrow, black-topped roads and walked up the rocky, tree-covered hollows, and he seemed very different from the man she'd known before.

He appeared to be genuinely interested in the people they saw and in what they had to say; he rarely mentioned his business or his plans. Lane still sensed his hard-driving energy just beneath the surface, but he spent less time at work, and when he was with her she could feel that his full attention was on the world she was showing him.

And on her. Although he respected the new parameters she had set, he often looked at her in a way that told her that his desire for her was as strong as ever. Once or twice he put his arm around her as they walked up a hill or over some rough ground, and the longing to feel his length against her rushed in to haunt her as it did so many nights when she finally fell, exhausted, into her bed. She held fast to her resolve, however, and he didn't try with words to persuade her to break it.

At first their conversations centered almost warily around the experiences they were sharing, but gradually, during the long drives along the winding mountain roads, they began to relax and talk about things that were more personal. They didn't mention their relationship, however. It was as if they had made an agreement not to touch verbally as well as physically.

Instead she told him something about her childhood, and they discussed their ideas about the arts and about life. It was almost as if they were beginning their relationship all over again, the getting acquainted stage coming before the physical, just the way she'd wanted, Lane thought.

One afternoon as they drove back into Covey they were having a particularly good conversation. Vance was lounging in the passenger seat, totally relaxed, his dark eyes gleaming with interest and satisfaction as he questioned her about Old Man Charlie, whom they had just taken home after a trip to Chalky Mountain to see a log church he'd helped his father build.

It felt so right to be with Vance, and so natural for him to appreciate the old man as she did, that she felt a flicker of real hope spring into life deep inside her, a hope that they could truly get to know each other. It was an idea that had been nagging at her for several days, one that she had been trying to suppress by filling every hour with more work than she could possibly get done and by disciplining herself not to even think about Vance except when she was with him.

She couldn't suppress it, though. No matter how much she ignored them, the ghosts of the passionate embraces they had shared were always hovering nearby when they were together. She wanted those embraces again; she wanted *him*. And maybe she could have him—if someday they could have a real understanding that pulled them together as strongly as their desire had always done.

The thought beat in her head and caused her pulse to quicken its rhythm. Blindly she parked the jeep in its usual place in Alice's side yard and silently rejoiced when he walked with her up the steps and onto the porch instead of going straight to his pickup truck as he usually did.

"Just think how long it must have taken for Charlie and his father to finish even that small church," he remarked as he sank onto the porch swing without waiting to be invited. "I'd always thought that all the neighbors came any time a building was put up and did it in a day."

"Well, from what Charlie says, his dad was too much of a perfectionist for that," she answered, sitting down in the swing beside him, feeling very close to him in the drowsy afternoon. The buzz of insects surrounded the house, and the honeysuckle that covered the trellises at each end of the porch laced its sweet fragrance into the air. The light was just beginning to dim as the sun dropped toward the top of Big Caney Ridge, and suddenly, as she looked at Vance's strong profile against the mountain's green purple background, the afternoon seemed too beautiful to bear.

Vance's next words destroyed it. "You know, Lane," he was saying, "I really think we should ask Charlie if we could use him in one of our ads for Greenbriar. He'd be perfect."

Disappointment twisted in her. Why did he have to ruin it all?

She pushed away her emotions, determined not to let them grow, and kept her voice very casual. "Vance, you know I couldn't approach him about anything like that. Any commercial suggestions from me would make everyone think that I'm using the information they give me to make money for myself."

"You wouldn't have to approach him—I would," he answered. "The ads wouldn't be making money just for me; Charlie would be paid well." He turned suddenly intense eyes to her. "He needs the money, Lane," he said. "That old man doesn't have a thing."

"But he doesn't see it that way," she said earnestly. "He lives in a beautiful place where his roots go back two hundred years; he has dozens of relatives all around him; he's free to do whatever he wants all day, every day. Charlie doesn't *need* any money."

The enthusiasm was growing now as his gaze captured hers; the old Vance was back—all business and driving ambition. "Listen, Lane, there are so many great ad ideas, not only in Charlie, but in almost everyone you've introduced me to these past few weeks. They're just what we need to get the rest of the world curious about and interested in coming to see the Cumberlands."

He pounded one fist lightly on his knee, his mind racing. "These people are colorful—they're different. Just think of the attention they'd attract saying 'y'all come' in a series of television commercials!"

"Haven't I been telling you . . ." She stopped in midsentence, distracted by a movement just inside the window that was only a foot or so from her end of the swing. "Rowena?" she called. "Is that you?" There was no answer. "I thought I got a glimpse of Rowena's red hair," she explained, peering into the dim house. "But I guess I was mistaken."

She turned back to Vance. "I've been telling you that these people are truly different," she said, "and now you're seeing it for yourself. I just hope that now you'll stop saying that the only unique thing about them is that they're twenty years behind the times!"

They went on to talk about Polly Clay and some of the other Appalachian people that she had introduced him to, and she steered the conversation to interesting bits of information about them, keeping it as far away from the ad campaign as she could. The day had been the best for her in a long, long time, and she wasn't going to let the end of it be spoiled. Vance knew how she felt, and she knew that no matter how interested in people he was, he was more interested in business. She knew that, but just for a little while she wasn't going to think about it at all.

Vance left while there was still enough daylight for him to look over the day's progress at Green-briar and finally, reluctantly, Lane left the balmy evening to go into the house. She opened the screen door to the wide entry hall and stepped into the darkening house.

Someone was coming out of the living room just as she entered; even in the duskiness there was no mistaking the glow of Rowena's gleaming hair.

"Rowena!" she exclaimed. "Hello! I thought I saw you in the living room a while ago."

As she spoke she switched on the lamp that stood near the telephone table beside the staircase. Its sudden yellow beam threw Rowena's face into relief; it was set in a terrible white mask—of anger, of hatred, of indifference. Lane couldn't name all the emotions she saw carved there.

"I was going to ask you to come out and meet Vance. . . ." She stopped.

Rowena looked into her eyes for one long, terrible moment, then turned and started rapidly up the stairs without a word.

Lane stood looking after her, memories of the hopes she'd had for the girl as an almost-sister flashing involuntarily through her head. She had no idea what she had done now, but if she could trust her instincts, that look Rowena had just given her said that those hopes were forever dead.

Lane woke from her nap well into the late afternoon feeling no more rested than she had when she'd lain down. She lay without moving for a few minutes, feeling almost drugged by the restless sleep and the quiet stillness that surrounded her. Her head ached, and she rubbed her temples, wishing she had an aspirin. If she got up to get one, though, she'd have to stay up and face the rest of the day.

She huddled on the bed, her cheek against the sweat-dampened pillow, and as soon as she was awake enough her thoughts went to Vance, the way they had been doing lately. She hadn't seen or heard from him since the day they'd gone to visit Old Man Charlie, but she couldn't keep from thinking about him, remembering his touch and his kisses, trying to decide which side of him was the real one.

His suggestion about Charlie and the commercial kept coming back to her, and she was afraid that he really was only a businessman plotting out ways to help himself. But the optimistic side of her insisted that maybe he *was* her new companion who was concerned about his new acquaintances, a companion with whom she could have a lot in common. She didn't know, and she wanted to wait as long as she could before she found out.

She replayed their afternoon talk in the swing, and she wondered again whether Rowena had been sitting inside the house listening to them. But why? If she had been there, why hadn't she answered when Lane called to her?

And why wouldn't she speak to Lane? She made every attempt to avoid her, and on the few occasions when that was impossible, she had given her that same look seething with loathing and then acted as if Lane didn't exist.

Lane pushed away the pillow as if her disturbing thoughts would go with it and tried to make her mind a blank. For two days it had been stubbornly refusing to stop looking for an insight into Vance's true nature and an explanation for Rowena's behavior; that was why she'd spent the past nights tossing in her bed or pacing the floor.

Finally she gave up trying to escape and reluctantly got up. She went to the bathroom and washed her face, then started downstairs. She met Rowena halfway up the staircase.

"Hi . . ." Lane began, but the hateful look slashed at her, and then Rowena took the rest of the stairs two at a time, as if she couldn't get away from Lane fast enough.

Lane stood looking after her for a minute, trying to control the quick impulse she'd had to follow the girl and shake her and shout at her until she explained her behavior. At last she looked down at her hands, their knuckles white with gripping the wood, and sudden tears of frustration stung her eyelids. She couldn't stand it anymore; she had to try to find out what was wrong and set it right.

She had avoided mentioning the problem to Alice because the woman already had enough worries about Rowena, but now she would. She had to do something.

She found Alice on the wide back porch, rocking while she shelled some early green peas into the faded print fabric of her apron. Lane smiled as she saw that Alice had brought a tin pan out of the kitchen for the peas, but was using her apron instead.

"That's exactly what Granny Belle used to do," she said, and was surprised to hear that her voice was unsteady. She waited a minute, then tried again. "She always had a pan or a bowl, but she never used it if she was wearing an apron."

"It's whatever you get used to," Alice replied with a little smile of welcome. "Just whatever's habit."

Her shrewd eyes fixed themselves on Lane, who sat down on the top step and turned to lean her back against the post of the porch railing. Lane sighed and looked out at the mountain; roiling clouds were gathering against it. That and the oppressive sultry air heralded a night of thunderstorms.

"Looks like we'll get some rain," she said, trying to think of a way to broach the subject of Rowena.

For a minute Alice didn't answer. Then she said abruptly, "What's the matter?"

"Rowena won't speak to me," Lane blurted, stating the problem more bluntly than she had intended to. "And it's driving me crazy. She hates me for something, and I don't know what—unless she still thinks I'm keeping Thad from her."

Silently she took the pan and began to fill it from the almost-full basket of peas on the floor by Alice's chair.

"If she wasn't so blind she could see that you're not," Alice said. "I don't know what's got into her now."

"Alice," Lane said, suddenly very still, "why don't you let her date him?" She felt her back tense in expectation of Alice's anger, but she had to go on. The only way to make Rowena see that she wasn't taking Thad from her was to give her a real chance with him. "I think Thad might get interested in Rowena if he had a little encouragement."

Alice didn't answer. The silence of the afternoon was underlined by the fact that there wasn't even a breath of a breeze. Lane had spoken in a normal tone, but for a minute she thought Alice hadn't heard.

The only sound for what seemed like a long time was the small, crisp snapping of the fresh green pea pods. Then Alice said, "It was a summer day, a day a whole lot like this one—you know, a day with a waiting in the air—when I first knew I loved him."

And she went on to tell Lane the story of how she had loved Thad Campbell's daddy and how he had broken her heart. The love and the happiness that had lasted nearly a year and the hurt that had lasted almost forty, the hurt that had outlived the man, were in her voice and her face and she poured all of them out to Lane.

"I never loved a man like I loved Jason Campbell," she concluded, dumping all the peas that filled her apron into the pan Lane held. "And no man ever hurt me like he did. I never could trust another one after that, and that's why I never did marry."

Lane was quiet. She felt that she had actually been feeling the joy and the grief the young Alice had lived through. And now she understood the older Alice.

"But, Alice, Thad isn't his father," she protested softly at last. "They're two different people. There's no reason to believe that he'd treat Rowena the way Jason treated you."

"He just might," Alice argued stubbornly. "He's the spitting image of him, and he's got the same devil in his eyes." She shook her head firmly, and when she spoke again the pain in her voice was fresh, as if Jason Campbell had just told her that he was marrying another woman.

"No," she said, "I just can't take the chance of letting that child go through what I went through." She busied herself with the peas and the basket, as if activity could banish the memories.

Lane sat very still, the round tin pan forgotten in her lap, her eyes on the dark gray clouds billowing down the side of Big Caney. Fear came to her, a fear that rode on this new understanding of how much a man could hurt a woman. But she wasn't thinking that Thad could hurt Rowena the way Jason had hurt Alice. When the first low roll of thunder rumbled across the valley she was thinking about herself and Vance Morgan.

Chapter Seven

The next morning Lane woke to the proverbial clear day after the storm. Bright sunlight flooded in through her window, and a pleasant breeze followed it, making the thin curtains seem to dance. She had actually slept well; the rain that had beaten against her window in the night had washed away her tension, and the long dream she'd had that she was in Vance's arms had banished her fears and left her irrationally happy. As she dressed in jeans and a pale blue knit top she hummed "Barb'ry Ellen," the mournful tune forming a counterpoint for her bubbly good feelings.

The phone rang as she started downstairs, and before she even reached it she knew that it was Vance. A morning like this couldn't exist unless he called.

His voice sang through her veins. "Lane, are you

free this morning?" he asked. "Late yesterday I ran into Charlie Campbell down in Covey, and he said if we'd come up there today he'd show us how to cut the different notches. Somebody brought him some logs."

"All right," she answered. "I suppose I could go." She was surprised at how calm she sounded.

"Great," he said. "I'll pick you up in half an hour."

She hung up the phone and stood staring at it for a minute, smiling at the perfection of the day and reveling in this manifestation of the good feeling of her dream. Finally, though, she gave herself a mental shake and tried to wake up. This was reality and that dream might never come to be. She'd better concentrate on her work.

As she went back up to her room she tried to think of what she should be doing to get ready for another visit to Charlie's, but she couldn't even decide what she needed to take with her. All she could think about was the fact that she was going to see Vance.

Finally, through sheer force of will, she organized the camera, film and notebooks in her leather bag and found a blank tape for the recorder. She had to stop this, she thought. Vance was probably just setting everything up so that he could try to get Charlie into one of his commercials; this didn't necessarily mean that he wanted to be with her.

When she answered the door and found him standing there on the porch, though, she could tell that he *did* want to be with her. The look glinting in his dark eyes was unmistakable, and the sunlight dancing off his black hair, still damp from the shower, was like a reflection of the excitement dancing along every nerve in her body.

She stood for a moment just looking at him, wanting nothing in the world but to reach up and run her fingers through his hair. He smiled into her eyes as if he knew that, and she dropped her lids to hide the thought.

He waited just inside the door while she got her things, and then they stepped out into the morning, dozens of shades of green sparkling all over the mountainsides. Vance touched her arm lightly as they went down the steps, and she felt as if she could float the rest of the way.

She suggested that they take her jeep, as they had been doing, but he brushed the idea away and led her to the pickup truck that he drove when he was overseeing the construction at Greenbriar.

It was as if he were taking complete control again, she thought, as he drove swiftly and confidently along the narrow highway toward Bittercreek Hollow. A wisp of the fear she'd felt the evening before came floating back to her. He'd just been humoring her these past few weeks by letting her drive him around in her jeep and show him things from her point of view. Now he was in charge again, and things were going to be done his way.

But *she* still had to be in control of one thing, she thought, forcing her eyes away from the outline of his chiseled profile and attaching them desperately to the green mountainside moving by so close beside her window. If she were going to survive she had to keep him from taking her in his arms again.

She forced her mind back to her work. "Charlie

must really have taken to you," she told him. "I'm surprised that he told you about this instead of calling me or getting word to me through Thad."

"No, I'm nothing but a messenger boy," he said, flashing her his sideways grin. "He just happened to see me walking along the street, and telling me was easier than calling you up. It's you he loves; he could care less about me."

She laughed lightly, but inside she trembled. The caressing tone of his voice was like the touch of his hand on her skin.

When they arrived at Bittercreek Hollow they found that Charlie, too, was in a mood to match the morning. After they had talked about the morning weather, the previous night's storm and how full they had found the creeks between Bittercreek Hollow and Covey, he led them around to his back yard, where several logs were stacked.

"I asked Sloan Watson, that's my sister's boy, to bring me these jist so I could show you what I been tellin' you about," he stated, picking up the axe that was lying on the back porch. "You can write this down for yore university a whole lot better if'n' you can see it done than if you jist hear about it."

He hewed two sides off two of the logs with hands that were surprisingly steady for his age and began to slope the top surface of one until it satisfied him. Then he rested the second log on it and looked at Vance, motioning toward the porch again.

"Git me that steel ruler, son," he said. "We've gotta mark this one now so's we can make 'em fit."

Vance did as he was asked and helped Charlie by holding the logs and ruler as he marked. The old man refused to let him handle the axe, however, and he hewed the second log himself until it fit snugly into the first.

"Now this here's the dovetail notch that my granddaddy and his pa used on our cabin," he said proudly when he had finished. "It's not only the purtiest of the notches I know, but it's the strongest. There's just somethin' about it—it'll pull ever one of the wall logs towards the inside of the house. That way none of 'em can kick out or roll."

Lane and Vance expressed their admiration for the intricate notch that really was beautiful; then Charlie went on to demonstrate the saddle notch and the "hog pen notch," which was commonly used in the mountains.

Lane had turned on her recorder when he began, and she took notes and several photographs at each stage of the demonstration. All the time, however, she had trouble keeping her attention on Charlie. Her eyes and her thoughts kept wandering to Vance: his long, strong fingers on the handle of the axe as he picked it up to give it to Charlie; the intensity of his attention as he concentrated on the process Charlie was showing them; his dark brown gaze taking in every detail of the finished product.

She wanted to be taking pictures of him, not of the lifeless wood. But she needed a movie camera for that—she wanted to capture the flowing, confident way he moved against the perfect green and yellow morning and keep it just for herself forever.

Once they were finished the completed notches somehow seemed to be the work of all three of them, and as they put away the tools and went into the simple cabin there was a strong feeling of accomplishment and camaraderie among them.

"You'ns stay and eat with me," Charlie invited them. "I've got a little something cooked that we can warm up."

Lane and Vance set the worn table with the ancient bone-handled utensils and tin plates, and Charlie warmed up beans, made a pan of corn bread and arranged some wilted lettuce and onions. They all ate as if they were starved, and then Charlie insisted that they go sit on the porch.

"Jist leave all that stuff right where it is," he ordered. "I've got nothin' else to do all day but clean it up. I'll do it when ye've gone."

He settled into his favorite rocker on the porch, and Vance and Lane shared the swing as they had done at Alice's. "This is getting to be a habit, isn't it?" Vance asked as they sat down, smiling at her as if that were the most marvelous secret in the world. Her heart turned over.

She had to stop; she had to stop thinking of him this way or she'd never be able to keep him at arm's length, she told herself.

She forced herself to look at Charlie, who had propped his feet up on the porch post. He reached into the bib pocket of his overalls for his tobacco pouch, fixing Lane with his sharp blue stare as he eased his fingers between the strings with the utmost care.

"They's a story that oughtta be wrote down," he said slowly, and the intensity in his tone made Lane suddenly alert. "We ain't never told it outside the family, but you're preservin' things, not blabbin' 'em all over creation."

Vance became still beside her, beginning to listen as hard as she was.

"My granddaddy and my daddy never wanted

this told, but I don't reckon they'd care if I'd tell it to you," Charlie went on. In spite of that reassurance, though, he hesitated.

He took a corncob pipe from his hip pocket and dipped it into the little sack. "Now don't you tell it to nobody—you jist go back to yore university and write it down," he ordered. "But I want it wrote down 'cause there's allus s'much fightin' in the world."

He struck a match and lit the tobacco, then pulled on the pipe. "I've never liked killin'," he said, as if that were explanation enough. "Not even game."

He held the pipe in one gnarled hand. "It was during the war between the Rebels and the Yankees," he began, "and all my folks was sympathizin' with the Rebels. So was jist about all the folks in this county.

"Well, we was sorta on the border, and there was fightin' around here in and out of the hills, sort of what they would call a guerrilla war, I reckon. There was 'bushwhackers,' too, that wasn't on either side but was jist wanderin' around robbin' and murderin'." He stopped to pull on the pipe again, his eyes fixed on the far distance. "It was dangerous to be out much, especially at night, 'cause you never knowed if whoever you run across would be friendly or not.

"Well, anyhow, my granddaddy and his brothers was ridin' with a band for the Rebels, and my grandma was livin' here with her sister. That was before she had any little 'uns.

"Somehow they got word that their brother had been shot over on Troublesome River." His attention came back to the present and he looked at them. "That's over north of here; it runs down from the high ridges across Impetuous Mountain."

He waited to see if they knew the exact location for this story that was so important to him. "It comes into a waterfall on the ridge above the gorge on the Little Caney. . . ." He gestured toward Vance with a quick movement of the pipe. "Not too fur from where you're buildin' yore park or whatever."

"We know the place," Vance said, nodding, and with a quick stab of recognition Lane realized that they were talking about the waterfall where she had met Vance.

"Well, one night my grandma and her sister— her name was Verna—they slipped out to see if they could find their brother. They drove a young mare hitched to a sled 'cause if he was hurt bad or was dead they'd have to haul him in.

"It took some time to get across to the Troublesome, and then they searched all up and down it for some sign that their brother was hidin' out. One of the places they looked was a cave they'd played in as kids; they thought he might've gone there."

Charlie stopped to light his pipe, which had gone out. His quick glance darted out from under the battered hat brim to see whether his audience was listening. They were, so he slipped back into the past.

"At first they thought they'd found him, 'cause there was somebody in the cave, all right, but when they got up close they seen it was a stranger. He was sick and about half delirious. They also seen he was a Yankee.

"Wal, at first they didn't know what to do, but it

was on to comin' daylight by then, and they knowed they couldn't find their brother that night. They jist didn't have the heart to go and leave the Yankee boy, though, so finally, after they'd worried it around some, they loaded him on the sled and brought him in.

"At first they'd told one another that they'd turn him over to the Rebels as soon as some of them come by, but by the time they'd took care of him for a day or two they knowed they wouldn't. But they didn't know where to put him, 'cause their menfolks come home from time to time and *they'd* see him, even if them women could keep him hid from the neighbors, which they probably couldn't.

"Wal, finally my granddaddy and his brothers come home for a day or two. The brother the women had heard was hurt had been shot, all right, but he was still ridin', and he was with them. They come in a'cussin' the Yankees, and the womenfolks was scared to death about the boy they had hid in the barn.

"Verna insisted on seein' to their horses that evenin' and them stayin' up at the house, and she and my grandma managed to keep their secret for that one more night. The news'd be out in the mornin', though, for some of the men would go to the barn then for sure.

"So, my grandma told me, sometime before mornin' she told my grandpa the whole story. She confessed it all to him, and he wasn't too upset because the boy had been sick when they found him. But the Yankee was well now, and he was all set to take him to the nearest Rebel officers and turn him in.

"Grandma jist couldn't give in to it, though. The

Yankee boy had been there for two weeks and he hadn't harmed her or Verna and now he was a friend. She pleaded with my grandpa and at last he gave in. He allus was plumb crazy about my granny.

"Wal, he was the oldest of his brothers, and his word was pretty much law. The next morning he told them all the whole story and said that when the fightin' had moved away from there they'd set the Yankee out to go home, but until then, no one was to tell a soul about him.

"None of them ever did, and he stayed there for nigh onto six months. When he left for home he said he'd send back for Verna someday, for he had fell in love with her."

Old Man stopped and drew on his pipe. He smoked it and looked into the hazy distance.

"Well?" Lane prompted. "Did he?"

The narrow blue eyes flashed to hers. He nodded. "Eyeh, he did," Charlie affirmed, the pipe stem between his teeth.

She waited for him to go on, but to him the story seemed to be finished.

"Charlie?" she asked. "Did Verna go?"

He shook his head. "Too fur," he said. "Way up in Pennsylvany somewheres. Couldn't go off like that and leave all her folks. She married one of the Clemsons."

After Charlie stopped speaking Lane was aware of Vance's arm along the back of the swing, lightly touching her shoulder as they absorbed what Charlie had told them. They sat quietly for a long while, just drinking in the afternoon, looking down the back slope toward the old barn sitting so solid in its patch of sunlight and wondering whether it was the same one that had sheltered the Yankee boy so long ago. Lane knew that Vance was sharing her thoughts just as surely as if he had said so; she didn't need speech. It was as if Charlie had spoken so many words that now they didn't need any more for a while.

The closeness that they had shared among the three of them was transformed into something private between her and Vance now. The two of them were together, thinking about that story of Charlie's, reliving it. The old man had gone away from them, his memories moving past his grandmother and on down the years between then and now that they knew nothing about.

The day was still as bright as it had been when she woke, and the whole world still seemed yellow and green. Charlie's cabin and barn were in a valley slightly wider than some, but the sides of the surrounding hills were still very close, and they cradled Lane and Vance in a timeless hollow of light and shade that held only the ghosts of the past and the scattered chirps and rasps of birds and insects.

After a very long time Vance stirred, glancing regretfully at the thin gold watch on his wrist. "Charlie?" he said. "Charlie, we ought to be going now."

The old man nodded without turning to them, his pipe clenched in his teeth, his eyes on the far distance. With his chair tilted back and his feet propped up on the post he was as still and weathered as if he were a part of the house itself, as if he, too, had been sitting in that very place for a hundred and fifty years. He didn't speak.

"I really have to get back," Vance said quietly to

Lane, an apologetic tone in his voice. "I have a meeting with some subcontractors at Greenbriar in an hour."

"It's all right," she answered. "I need to get going, too."

She touched Charlie lightly on the shoulder as they passed him. "'Bye, Charlie," she said softly, but his only answer was an almost imperceptible nod of his head.

Vance drove much more slowly on the way back to Covey, almost as if he resented having the appointment to meet, she thought. The windows of the pickup were down, and she watched the breeze play in his hair and looked at his chiseled profile against the light, as if looking at him could comfort her for not touching him.

"It's a completely different world, isn't it?" he asked from the depths of his reverie. "I can't even imagine what it'd be like to live in the same house all my own lifetime, much less in the same house where my father and grandfather had lived." He took his eyes from the road to look at her, to demand a confirmation of what he was saying.

She nodded. "I know. I couldn't believe how the past and the present seemed to run together while he was talking. Couldn't you almost see Verna going to the barn to check on the Yankee soldier?"

He answered with a nod.

"I love it," she went on thoughtfully, almost to herself. She sighed. "I never lived in the same place for six months all the years when I was growing up, and I really don't even know my parents, much less my grandparents and great-grandparents."

His eyes were mere slits as he squinted against

the lowering sun. "My dad disappeared when I was five, and I can barely remember him," he said, the careful, impersonal tone in his voice contrasting with his words. "And my mom was gone all the time, trying to scrape together enough to feed us and pay the rent on that rat hole of an apartment. If anyone ever grew up without supervision, my brothers and I did. I guess it's a miracle that we aren't all in prison right now."

His words shocked her, and a sharp sympathy twisted in her stomach. She had been feeling sorry for herself, but her own childhood must have been heaven compared to what he had told her in those few terse sentences. Without thinking she reached out to him, her fingers brushing his cheek, but she said nothing.

He gave no sign that he noticed. "And money means nothing to Charlie," he went on, thinking aloud. "I'll bet he hasn't spent five minutes of his life trying to figure out how to make a buck."

"Oh, I don't know," she argued, switching her thoughts from him to Charlie with an effort. "He used to work in the mines some, and he was the mailman for a long time. After all, he raised a family, and they had to have food and clothes."

"But that's different from always scrambling for more," he said. "From thinking about money and working all the time, and no matter how much you have, never being able to make enough. Like I watch my brothers doing."

"And you?" she asked softly, her pulse beating harder as the words slipped out. She didn't want to make him angry, but she needed to know what drove him, what had made him push her against her will that night to help Gloria—just after his lips and his hands had promised her anything in the world that she wanted.

"Me?" he asked wearily, as if he had been asking himself that question over and over again. "It's not that," he said thoughtfully after a moment. "I've got enough. I don't know. . . ." He ran one long, tanned hand restlessly through the rich blackness of his hair. "Maybe it's the challenge." He gave her a quick, very direct glance. "Or maybe I just don't know what else to do," he said rapidly, almost as if he were embarrassed at revealing so much.

There was a trust beneath his discomfort, though, and suddenly the moment was more intimate than any they had ever shared; the closeness they'd been feeling all day was growing into an almost tangible bond between them. A painful excitement spread through her with the realization that as it drew her to him, it pulled down still another section of the wall she had built against him.

They were quiet as he pulled the pickup onto the narrow blacktop highway, and then he shifted the conversation back to Charlie as smoothly as he shifted the gears of the truck.

"But he needs *some* money," he said. "He's old and he might get sick, and that cabin's a long way from a doctor or a hospital." He put his elbow in the window frame and settled back into the seat. "In fact, that story he told us today could make him enough money so he'd have a little cushion. Why'd he say not to tell it to anyone?" He glanced at her, his brown eyes puzzled. "What is it that needs to be kept secret?"

"His family hid an enemy soldier and didn't turn him in," she explained. "It wasn't quite so bad to take in a sick man, but they kept him even after he got well and then let him go back to his own army unharmed. That was treason, disloyalty to their neighbors, who never even knew there was an enemy in their midst."

"But that was way over a hundred years ago, for God's sake!" he said, exasperated. "What difference does it make who knows it now?"

"A hundred years ago is still part of the family to Charlie," she tried to explain. "Remember how he said his daddy and his granddaddy didn't want that told?"

He nodded.

"Well, he's still loyal to them, just as loyal as he is to the members of his family who're still alive. It's all an ongoing thing—time, family, the stories, the legends and, above all, the loyalty. He's not going to do something to shame them, even if they aren't here to be embarrassed. You're always saying that he doesn't have anything, but he has his family name, which is even more important than money. The family comes before everything up here, and people not only would have a reason to criticize his grandfather, they'd think poorly of Charlie for telling the story now."

She looked out through the curving windshield, down the narrow, winding road that was the only one connecting Covey to the outside world. "It's a wonder that he ever told us."

"Why do you think he did?" he asked, his voice sharp with interest.

"Because he's thinking about dying and he wants it written down somewhere. To him it proves that people who are enemies don't always have to kill each other, and he wants that fact preserved."

She looked into his eyes and suddenly she felt deluged, flooded with the intensity of her feelings for Old Man Charlie and for Vance, who was trying so hard to understand him.

"Charlie recognizes that his grandfather was a compassionate man, but Charlie's friends wouldn't agree with that, don't you see?" she went on. "They'd say Charlie's granddaddy was a traitor for not killing the Yankee and a fool for listening to a woman's pleas for the man's life. His granddaddy would be seen as disloyal to his people, and around here that's the worst thing that can be said about anybody."

He nodded agreement, but as they pulled up in front of Alice's house he said, "It's just so hard to understand." He shook his head wonderingly. "This is ancient history."

"Well, yes and no," she answered. "Even if hardly anybody cared, if only one of Charlie's cronies passed judgment, Charlie would always regret that he'd told the story; he'd feel he'd betrayed his family and sullied his grandfather's memory."

He turned off the motor and sat looking down at her, the smile that curved his lips reflected in his eyes. "I'm just so glad I have you to explain all this to me," he said. "I'd never manage around here on my own."

All of the special closeness of the day and the understanding they had shared over the past weeks were in his voice. His feelings called to her, caressing her senses like a fulfillment. She moved a little closer to him before she realized what she was doing.

Then she knew it: She still wanted him; she

wanted him more than ever, and if he didn't leave her soon she'd be lost. She'd be in his arms once more, under his spell again, and the last remnants of the wall around her heart would be broken into bits.

"Don't walk me in, Vance," she heard herself saying, although what she really wanted to say was "Come in with me, Vance, come in and stay with me." She wanted to touch him so badly that she hurt, so she clasped her hands to keep them away from him, though her arms ached with the effort.

She looked down at her watch to get her eyes away from him, too. "You're going to be late for your meeting," she told him. "You'd better run."

He didn't answer, and she looked up into his eyes. They were deep and dark, as mysterious as the forests they brought to her mind, and they glinted with the light she'd seen the first day she met him, the light that looked into her very soul.

"Lane, let's go up there tomorrow and look for the cave where they found the soldier," he suggested in a voice so rich with sensual promise that a shiver went through her. "We haven't been back to our waterfall since that very first day."

She sat very still under the double spell of his velvet voice and his captivating eyes. He was leaning toward her, totally relaxed, his arm resting along the back of the seat to lightly touch her shoulders. She knew that he was asking her for much more than his words expressed. If she went with him back to the waterfall she would go into his arms again, and this time he would come into her heart.

For one long beat of her pulse she tried to find the words to refuse him, but she searched every corner of her mind and found that they just weren't in her. Finally she nodded.

His hand slipped behind her head then, into the heavy mass of her hair, and he turned her face up to his. "I know you told me not to do this," he growled, "but I've obeyed you as long as I can."

His lips came down on hers sweetly, almost gently, and he began placing tiny kisses along the outline of her mouth, the space of a heartbeat between each one. She felt the now-familiar heat of wanting him begin to build in the very center of her being, and involuntarily her lips parted and her hands moved to the broad shoulders that formed a barrier between her and the rest of the world.

His mouth moved away from hers, however, and she stifled a little moan of disappointment. In compensation he kissed her softly over and over again; her cheekbones, her eyelids, the edges of her hair, moving very slowly as if he were afraid of frightening her.

Desire flamed in her, and her hand moved up to caress the side of his strong neck, then hungrily it traced the opening of his shirt to touch his muscular chest. It slipped beneath the cloth and moved over the muscular expanse, the crisp dark hairs curling against the sensitive skin of her open palm like dry brush to feed the fire.

He gasped as she found one flat nipple, and his lips came back to take hers with a hunger born of frustration and a passion denied for too long. His tongue traced her lips, then thrust against them to demand its way back into the sweetness that it had possessed before. It explored every corner of her sensitive mouth, and her own tongue came to meet it, caressing and welcoming it, breaking the last resistance she'd had into sparkling fragments of sensation that burst in her veins.

Finally he pulled away, and when she opened her eyes his were caressing her with the same hunger that had been in his kiss. For a long time he looked at her, as if he had lost his will to move, then at last he spoke. His voice was low and husky as it had been that night by the lake. "Tomorrow at ten," he said. "I'll pick you up here."

She was into the house and halfway up the stairs when she realized that she was almost light headed from the bubbling joy pulsing through her veins. Vance was her friend now, and he still wanted her. He had kissed her again in that special way; he, too, still felt the heat of the fire between them that the past weeks had not put out. And he had said "our" waterfall!

She stopped, totally still, her eyes fixed on the bright colors of the quilt blocks Alice had hung at intervals up the staircase, her hand on the smooth old wood of the railing.

Her heart hadn't waited for the next day and the trip to the waterfall. It had already taken him in.

Chapter Eight

Jane leaned back against the smooth bank of earth that curved around the picnic spot they'd chosen and crossed her legs Indian-style. She was pulsing with excitement, with a pure joy that she couldn't remember feeling since some vague occasion in her childhood. All night and all the way up the mountain that morning she had felt it: a nameless happiness that made the very air she breathed something to savor.

She watched Vance's long form as he stretched out across the other side of the blanket they had spread over the coolness of the forest floor. The confident way he moved and the woodsy tones of his dark hair and eyes above the dark green shirt he wore made him fit right into the background, she thought. He reminded her of a wild animal who lived there in the woods.

"There's not a cave within a hundred miles of here," he declared, sinking onto the ground with a sigh of pretended exhaustion. "You've worn me out looking for something that doesn't exist."

"And whose suggestion was this?" she countered, laughing. "I seem to remember that *you* wanted us to come up here and look for the cave where they found the Yankee soldier."

"Did I?" he asked, his sideways glance teasing her. "Well, I must have had some other reason in mind, too. If I didn't, we'll have to think of something, because obviously neither the cave nor the soldier is here."

He propped himself up on one elbow and turned to face her, his grin holding all the charm that came so naturally to him when he wanted to use it. His eyes held hers, their dark depths filled with challenge. "Any ideas?"

Her heart skipped a beat, then began a long, slow rhythm, and her eyes clung to his. The awareness of each other that they'd had the day before, the passion that had been in their kiss, was out in the open again.

It had been pulsing beneath the talk and the laughter and the light touches they had shared during the climb up to the falls and their halfhearted search for the cave Charlie had told them about. It had been mixed with—or the cause of?—the joy she was feeling, and now it was a palpable presence between them.

She looked back at him for an endless moment, the beat of her heart so strong and so hard that she thought her breath would stop.

Then she moved forward and reached for the

woven basket that his housekeeper had packed. "How about lunch?" she said quickly, her voice trembling a little.

He nodded slowly. "That's one possibility."

She opened the basket, but he didn't sit up to help her with it. He just lay very still, watching every movement of her hands and body with a hunger that had nothing to do with food.

She didn't look at him, but the weight of his eyes on her hands slowed her movements, already clumsy with the desire beating in her veins. The red-checked tablecloth was on top. She fumbled with it and took it out, and she was reaching for the wine cooler when his voice stopped her as surely as if his hand had taken hers.

"But I have another idea," he said quietly, only the huskiness of his voice betraying the fact that he wasn't merely continuing their conversation. "Let me help you put that away."

He sat up, and in one fluid movement he moved the basket and its contents off the blanket and into a patch of bird's-foot violets beside the little rock ledge that ran between them and the gorge that held the tumbling waterfall.

His hand brushed hers when he took the basket, and it came back to hers as if to a beginning. He leaned toward her to look into her eyes, but she bent her head and let her long hair fall between them as his hand gently followed the length of her arm and moved across her shoulder to find the sensitive lobe of her ear.

He caressed it, then stroked her neck, putting his other hand under her chin to turn her face up to his. He held her eyes with a gaze so strong that it drew her to him across the small space that still separated them, and at last she was sitting in the curve of his body, her back against his long, bent legs.

The only thought she had was that she had been waiting so long for this, and as she absorbed his touch even that faded away into the natural fulfillment that was part of the day.

His strong fingers traced the line of her jaw, the heart shape of her face, the strong cheekbones, her arched brows.

"You're so full of life," he said, very low. "I saw it the day we met. That day with this roaring waterfall and the yellow flowers that matched your hair." His hand cupped her head, holding it back against his knee with a strength that was almost fierce. "That day you made me feel something for the first time in years—you made me feel that just living could be a passionate experience."

His voice was harsh with longing, and he devoured her with his eyes for what seemed to her an endless time. Every inch of her, every nerve cell in her body, was aware, awake for the first time in her life. She was truly alive at last, and she was alive because of Vance Morgan.

He put his arms around her then and laid her back on the ground hungrily, his lips finding hers with a desperate sureness. Her mouth opened to his tongue instinctively, and she took it in with a longing that came from her soul.

He pressed her against his length as if it were impossible to hold her close enough, and her body, now clamorously eager for his, arched against him with a yearning that made her tremble. Her hands roamed over his back and then down over the slim curves of his hips.

They came back to his waist, reaching under his belt to pull at his shirt. She had to feel his skin under her hands; she couldn't think about anything else. When she had tugged the shirt free she ran her hands under it, her palms starving for the smoothness of his back. Her touch roamed over the muscular expanse and across the width of his shoulders, memorizing every beautiful line of him. She stroked his neck, then trailed her fingers in a gossamer caress down his spine to the hollow in the small of his back.

He made a deep, guttural sound—a wanton growl—and his mouth left hers to bury itself in her hair while his thumb took its place. Hungrily it traced the outline of her lips while his big hand cradled her head. Then his hand moved over the curve of her throat to trace a winding path between the crisp edges of her plaid shirt and into the valley between her breasts. She gasped and let her head fall back against his arm.

In one flowing motion he pulled her shirt open and undid the fastener of the wisp of lace beneath it. She tried to look at him, to see the wanting in his eyes, but her eyelids were too heavy with desire. The throbbing need that filled her was a drug; it was so powerful that she couldn't move at all.

She felt his hands at the zipper of her jeans, then heard and felt the swish of fabric. In moments her clothes and his were gone, and her long legs were entwined in his longer ones, every inch of her skin clinging to his and drinking in the sensation as if she were dying of thirst.

"You are so sexy," he murmured against her ear, his lips and his tongue caressing it, rousing her desire for him to a fever pitch. "You're not only beautiful, you're a sexy, sexy woman."

Now she could move again; she *had* to move against him. All of her body had to take in every bit of him that she could absorb. She ran her hands over his back, his shoulders, down the smooth length of his muscular legs.

His hands moved over her as if in answer. They stopped to cup her breasts briefly; they stroked the curve of her waist and flat stomach, caressed her thighs as if he would imprint every curve, every line, of her into his palms.

Then his lips were against her naked breast, and she uttered a little cry, a tiny sound of pleading that escaped from her with the last breath she could consciously take. She lay galvanized, breathless, as his lips traced the outline of her nipple and came back to the center to capture the hard, rosy tip between them and his tongue.

She gasped and cried out. Her hands flew from his shoulders to his neck, then up into his hair to keep him there, to keep him from ever taking that piercing pleasure away.

Even so, he finally did take it away, but when he did he replaced it with another delight that was even stronger, one that melded his body into hers with a fire that opened every pore of her skin. It was a pleasure that touched her and freed her from all the rest of the world, a pleasure that captured her totally and began an ache in her that she thought would tear her apart.

He trembled, too, and he whispered her name, his warm breath in her ear fanning the flame inside her until the fire built and built and she didn't think she could bear it. It would consume her. This marvelous rapture was never going to end, it was never going to let her go, but she didn't care. All she wanted was to be filled with him, to move with him forever.

She didn't know how long there was nothing in the world except her need and his, and she didn't know how their bodies could melt any closer together. But when the long spiral up to delight began, she brought him even nearer and gripped his shoulders with a fierceness she hadn't known she possessed.

When at last they reached its zenith and she cried his name out loud the fire that burned in her was purified into one golden flame that settled the stillness of its molten happiness into every cell of her body.

For a long time afterward they lay entwined, hardly stirring. She nestled her head into the hollow at the center of his chest, feeling as if her bones had melted, as if she would never want to move again.

She lay without thinking, letting the rushing water of the falls beat its rhythm into her body through the bluff of rock that towered above the river's bed. The spring world of yellow and green was wrapped around them, and as she moved her eyes over it, the shape of every tree, every rock, the formation of the very hillsides, welcomed and cradled her. She fit into Vance's side feeling that they were one person, and also that they both were one with the earth beneath them.

A long branch of a big birch beckoned from the other side of the falls, its tiny yellow leaves like stars against the backdrop of the water. She watched it signaling to her gently in the small breeze that was wandering lightly through the hills. The narrow stream of water shimmered like transparent ribbons over the layers of dark, greenish brown rock beneath, their color changing constantly in the light from blue to white to gray.

She had never felt so much a part of any place in the world as she did at that moment, and as her eyes touched the ledges where they had looked for the cave, she thought of Verna and her refusal to leave these hills to go to the Yankee soldier.

Yesterday she'd thought she understood that decision; she'd thought that if she'd had a family like that, then she would probably have done the same thing. Today, though, she didn't understand it at all.

Suddenly, in a flash of insight, she knew why. It was Vance's arms and not the mountains that were home to her now.

"But, Alice, I don't *remember* how to get to Tenlogs," Lane said, balancing her leather tote bag on one knee and searching through it furiously. "And I don't remember what I did with those photographs of the quilts that I wanted to ask Polly about."

And I'm lucky to even remember my own name, she thought with a smile. The previous day had filled her mind and her life with Vance, and now it was a wrench to come back to her everyday world. She felt as if she'd just returned from traveling to another continent.

One by one she took out the things that *were* in

the bag and piled them on the kitchen table: her camera, a fresh notebook, the tape recorder and a package of blank tapes.

"Now don't be covering up the table," Alice ordered. "I'm gonna fix you something to eat, even if you did miss breakfast."

"No, no," Lane protested absently as she turned the empty bag upside down and shook it. The pictures weren't there. "I'm in a hurry—Polly's waiting for me."

Unperturbed, Alice brought a steaming mug of coffee to the table. "Polly's probably been up since sunrise, taking out her quilts and spreading them out, straightening up her house and getting all dressed up for you to take her picture," she said. "Ten minutes more won't make any difference."

"Oh, no! Do you really think she has?" Lane wailed. "I'm so sorry! I should've gotten up earlier."

"Now, you didn't tell her you'd be there at sunup. It's just that she's getting older, and old people get impatient when something exciting is planned that day," Alice said over her shoulder as she went back to the counter. "I made fried pies early this morning. Sit down here and eat one. Relax for a minute."

She brought a large platter of golden brown, crescent-shaped pies to the table and transferred one to a small plate for Lane, who quickly put her things back into the bag. Alice went back for her own cup of coffee, then sat down opposite Lane.

"Now don't forget to ask Polly if she's done with the green and white Delectable Mountains," she said. "You'll never see a prettier quilt than that one."

"If she's finished, shall I remind her that you want it in the shop?" Lane asked, biting into the delicious tartness of the warm peach filling.

"No, she knows that," Alice answered. "If she thinks I'm pushing her, or telling her what to do, she'll keep it."

"Okay," Lane agreed. "I won't mention it." She took a sip of coffee. "I'm so disappointed that I can't find my pictures, though. I really wanted to show them to her and see if she has alternate names for the patterns or any stories about their history that I don't have."

"You can go back again later," Alice reassured her. "You've been to see Polly before, and she likes you, or she wouldn't have said she'd talk for your tape machine. More than likely, she'll ask you to the next quiltin', and you can take the pictures then and talk to everybody there."

Lane asked Alice to repeat the directions to Polly's house while she finished eating, and then she rose and picked up her bag.

"I hope she won't be all worn out with waiting," she said, giving Alice an affectionate hug good-bye as she started for the door. "I'll get up there as fast as I can and stay as long as she'll let me, so she won't feel that she went to all that trouble for nothing."

She stepped out onto the front porch and stopped for just a moment to take in the summer morning. No matter how much in a hurry she was, she could never resist that feeling of a new beginning that she always had in summer before the real heat of the day came in—that sensation that the whole world was warm and welcoming and the myriad shades of green that covered the mountains had been blended just for her.

That was even easier to believe since she and Vance had made love by the waterfall, she thought. A sharp wish shot through her—a wish that he were beside her, that he could share this moment with her, too.

She stared into the distance for a minute, letting the delicious memories wash over her again; then she shook them off and started down the steps. She had work to do.

Then she saw the van. It was parked just past the edge of Alice's yard, facing in the same direction as her own jeep, and it seemed to hold three or four people, all of whom were looking at her.

As she watched, the woman in the passenger side of the front seat got out and came toward her. She knew the woman, but for a split second she couldn't think who she was; this was such an alien setting for the stylish brunette. Then she realized: It was Gloria Sullivan.

"Lane! How nice to see you!" Gloria was saying, her hand outstretched in greeting. "I was beginning to worry that somehow we'd missed you this morning."

Lane just stood, staring at Gloria, who wore form-fitting designer jeans and high-heeled boots, astounded as much by Gloria's words as by the fact that she was there at all. Finally she said, "Gloria, what do you mean? What are you doing here?"

"Going with you to meet some of your fascinating mountain people, of course," the woman replied, her brown eyes sparkling innocently, as if she had actually received a warm invitation.

"You aren't going anywhere with me," Lane

shot back, anger blotting out her surprise and beginning to build inside her. "I thought I made that clear the first time the subject came up."

"But, Lane, dear," Gloria began to explain breathlessly, "Vance tells me that you're going to see a quilt-maker this morning, and that would be *so* colorful in our campaign. I've brought along a crew to film your interview with her, and later we'll show it to her and ask her permission to use it.

"Just think how great the ads will look—a quilt in bright colors draped on the faded wall of an old cabin, your little lady in front of it making another one, looking up from her work to urge people to come to the Cumberlands and visit Greenbriar. Wouldn't that just be perfect?"

With one part of her mind Lane heard every word Gloria said, but on another level she couldn't take in anything past "Vance tells me." Blood was pounding in her ears, and a terrible uncertainty began to thread through the anger that was shaking her. What was Vance doing? Was he still thinking that Gloria's work was so much more important than hers that he was encouraging this? Was Gloria that much more important to him than she was?

Too angry to answer, Lane turned away and swung up into the jeep, turning the ignition key almost before she was seated. She gunned the motor and headed out into the narrow road, questions tearing at her. When had Gloria come back? When had she seen Vance?

Quickly she went back over the evening before. She and Vance had stayed on the mountain by the waterfall, eating the picnic lunch and talking quietly, just enjoying each other until late afternoon. Reluctantly they had made the climb down to his truck before the light failed and driven dreamily through the gathering darkness back to Covey. He hadn't wanted to take her to Alice's; he'd asked her to go with him to the house on the lake, but she had refused. She'd wanted to be alone to try to understand all that had happened to her in that one afternoon, to examine the hold that he had taken on her heart.

So he surely hadn't been expecting Gloria, she thought, downshifting in preparation for the rise that led up to the main highway. She glanced in her rearview mirror before she pulled out and saw that the van was right behind her. He hadn't been expecting Gloria, but maybe she'd been there when he got home. Maybe *she'd* stayed at the lake house last night.

Hurt twisted in her, and she pushed down on the accelerator. The magic green morning was now totally gray; the tiny fringed phacelia blossoms that covered the forest floor almost down to the edge of the road were nothing but a chilling white blur as she sped past. She wished she could lead the van up some remote hollow to a dead end and leave Gloria and her helpers there forever.

She couldn't play games, though; she had to go to Polly's. The woman had been expecting her all morning and she didn't have a phone, so Lane couldn't call and explain. She'd have to go ahead and follow her schedule, explaining to Polly and trying to act as if Gloria weren't even there. If she couldn't get rid of her, she would ignore her.

And she would ignore the doubt and the hurt that were slashing at her. If she thought about Vance now she'd never be able to get through the interview.

The rest of the way up to the little community called Tenlogs, Lane tried to concentrate on her work. Mentally she listed the questions she wanted to ask Polly and she tried again to think where those elusive photographs might be, but by the time she pulled up in front of Polly's cabin more than half of her attention was still on the white van behind her.

True to Alice's prediction, Polly was sitting on her porch, neatly dressed, just waiting.

Lane smiled at her and waved, but before she could call to her, Gloria's van had pulled up between them and Gloria had bounced out. By the time Lane gathered up her things and reached the porch Gloria was introducing herself to Polly and signaling to her crew to get out with their cameras.

"You didn't tell me you was bringing people with you," Polly greeted Lane, accusation in her quiet tone and somber eyes.

"Polly, I'm so sorry," Lane said. "They aren't with me. They just followed me up here; I didn't bring them."

"I don't like strangers comin' up to my place," the old woman went on, her body and voice stiff. She was standing now, defensive.

"I think they're harmless," Lane said, trying to reassure her. "They just want to take some pictures of you and your quilts, but you don't have to let them."

Polly's brown eyes surveyed the scene again, darting from one to the other of the cameras that Gloria's young men were setting up. "No, I don't," she agreed sharply. "I'm not aimin' to be in no moving picture."

"Could you bring out one or two of your quilts,

please, Mrs. Clay?" Gloria called as she supervised the placement of the cameras. "We'll just hang one of the brightly colored ones right behind your chair there, and you can sit down and talk to Lane about how you made it." She came toward the porch. "Do you have a quilt in progress right now that you could bring out, too? It'd be great to really see your technique in action."

Polly stared at her as if she were a particularly noxious weed that had just sprung up in her garden and then without a word she turned to go into the house. For a second Lane thought she intended to exclude her, too, but the old woman held the screen door open until Lane had passed through, then latched it firmly behind them and walked on into the back of the house.

Gloria knocked firmly, as if to say that they had forgotten her.

Lane looked at her through the screen. "Go away, Gloria," she said. "You'll never get an interview with Polly now, and I may not, either." Her eyes bored into Gloria's and they willed her, *ordered* her, to leave.

Gloria stared back for a minute, hating to admit defeat. "Oh, she may come back out in a few minutes when she gets used to the idea," she replied, trying to make her tone light. "Why don't you see if you can talk her into it, Lane?"

She smiled sweetly, trying one last time to use her charm, but Lane's face remained an angry mask, and finally Gloria looked away, glancing at her alert young men with their useless equipment.

"We'll just hang around for a little while and see," she said.

"You'll be wasting your time," Lane replied shortly. She turned away and went to find Polly, who was in the enormous bare room at the back of her house where her quilting frame was set up.

"I've got to git to work," the old woman announced briskly. "I've done wasted the biggest part of the mornin'."

She put on her thimble and wrapped a bandage around her thumb to protect it from the pricks of the needle, her movements quick and efficient but edged with irritation.

She didn't sit down, though; she stood leaning on the ladder-backed chair beside the quilting frame, her lips drawn tight in disgust. Her eyes flashed to Lane's. "That woman has more brass than anybody I've ever seen!" she declared. "Who in the world is she anyhow?"

"Her name is Gloria Sullivan. She's from New York, and she's down here making advertisements," Lane explained.

"Advertisin' what?"

"Greenbriar Amusement Park," Lane admitted reluctantly. She hoped that Polly would forget that the park was Vance's. Polly had liked Vance when Lane had brought him by, and she didn't want to ruin that.

There was another reason for not wanting to think about the extent of Vance's involvement in this fiasco, she admitted to herself. A personal reason. The tension that had been forming in her stomach all the way up to Polly's was crushing her lungs until she could hardly breathe.

She pushed the thought down again and glanced around her. In the next room she could see dozens of quilts spread out, some on the bed, some on the big blanket chest, and some on chairs, their colors and patterns overlapping.

"Are we going to make that tape today, Polly?" she asked. "I see you have a lot of your quilts out for me to see."

"Law, no, that'll have to wait 'til some other time," Polly answered, nervously taking her thimble off and leaving it in the middle of the tautly stretched fabric. "I see I'm too riled up to quilt and neither do I like showin' off my work when I'm all upset. It's like makin' yeast bread. I can't have nothin' to do with it unless my kitchen's clean and my mind's settled."

Somehow the way she spoke seemed terribly final to Lane, and she felt a sudden despair, as if she would never get the tape she had been wanting to get so badly. She had built up to this interview with three previous visits, and now it was ruined. She would have to wait several more days for it, *if* she got it at all.

The sound of the van's motor being started floated in through the open door, and Polly tilted her head to listen. "Sounds like she's given up," she remarked, deep satisfaction in her tone. "You need to tell that Vance feller that that pushy woman's liable to ruin his business."

Polly's words rang in Lane's ears a few minutes later as she maneuvered the jeep along the rutted road out of the hollow. She should have known that Polly wouldn't forget the connection between Vance and Greenbriar, and she couldn't forget it any longer, either.

The winding road ahead of her blurred as tears welled up in her eyes. Was the closeness that had been growing between her and Vance nothing but a fantasy? Had yesterday been nothing but another conquest for him? Just a pleasant respite from his busy schedule?

She came out of the mouth of the hollow and crossed the narrow creek to get to the highway. She waited for two coal trucks to pass, and when she pulled onto the two-lane blacktop she turned in the opposite direction from Covey. She headed toward Jackson Lake.

Vance had to know that Gloria had ruined a morning's work for her and could have alienated Polly entirely.

And *she* had to know whether he was still the same man he had been the day before.

Chapter Nine

$\mathcal{T}$he ubiquitous white van was sitting in the spacious driveway of the house on the lake, and as soon as Lane saw it she became furious all over again. She got out of the jeep and went up the walk with quick, indignant steps, the sound of her clogs on the stones of the path echoing hollowly in time with the angry thudding of her pulse.

The housekeeper opened the door almost as soon as she rang, and when she indicated that Vance was in his office Lane strode purposefully toward its open door without waiting to be announced.

He was seated behind the big desk, absorbed in a computer printout that was unfolded in front of him. The sleeves of his pale blue shirt were rolled up, and his muscular forearms rested on some of the dozens of papers that covered almost every inch of the broad desktop.

Lane stared at his hands, and the hard kernel of hurt that had been in her throat all morning threatened to choke her. Those were the same hands that had caressed her the day before; they had been almost a part of her own body, she thought wildly. Now they belonged to a stranger.

Gloria was just behind Vance, putting a mock-up of an ad on an easel. There were several other stiff posterboard rectangles scattered around. They occupied two of the chairs, and three of them were standing on the floor, leaning against one wall.

Well, she certainly didn't waste any time once she finally left Polly's, Lane thought. Gloria is nothing if not efficient.

"Vance, may I talk with you?" For a second Lane couldn't believe that the voice cutting across the silence was hers. The tension, the bitterness, in it made it an alien sound.

His eyes met hers, startled at first, then glowing with pleasure at seeing her. "Lane!" he said, rising. "Of course, come in."

"Hi, Lane," Gloria said stiffly. "Did you get your interview?" She wore a vague air of martyrdom, as if her work of the morning had been ruined because of Lane's selfishness.

Lane merely glanced at her. Then, without answering, she looked back at Vance. "Alone, I mean," she said harshly.

He looked mystified at the commanding tone in her voice, then annoyed. His eyes darkened a shade. "If you could wait five minutes. We've just set up these ads, and I need to approve them today. My afternoon is booked solid, so we have to do it now."

"Of course," she replied coldly. "I should have

realized that Gloria's work would take precedence over everything else. After all, you think it's so important that you've let it ruin mine."

He frowned, his eyes puzzled. "What are you talking about?" His voice was sharp now. Her tension and antagonism were apparently contagious.

"About the fact that you sent Gloria to follow me and try to push her way into filming my interview with Polly this morning!" She took a deep breath to keep her voice from trembling. "And that ruined it! Polly was in no mood to make a tape—instead she was frightened and angry at being invaded by strangers. Now I doubt very much that I can ever get her to agree to a formal interview again!"

She felt tears edging into her eyes, but she held them back through sheer force of will and looked from Vance to Gloria and back again. "I told you. I've told you both over and over again that I don't want any commercial overtones affecting my work." She swallowed hard. "And you simply cannot accept that." Her eyes held Vance's, the fury and betrayal she felt putting a hardness into hers that was as unyielding as the implacability in his.

His hard gaze flicked to Gloria. "You followed her up to Polly Clay's?"

"Yes," Gloria admitted, in a tone that implied that anyone else would certainly have done the same thing. "If you want to use photographs of real people instead of models, I have to get started immediately. We need to get this campaign kicked off."

Vance nodded, running his hand worriedly

through his hair and looking back down at the papers he'd been immersed in. He picked up the printout again and frowned at it. Lane could see now that it was covered with numbers.

"I know we do," he said thoughtfully. "We need to get it kicked off and we need to make it really good. We're so far behind schedule on the construction end that when we finally do open the ads'll have to bring in half the country to make up for the delay."

Gloria touched his shoulder, then patted it sympathetically. She was standing very close to him, looking into his face. "Don't worry, Vance," she said, her voice very soft, caressing him. "We can pull it off."

Lane's stomach twisted. Vance glanced away from the numbers then, and up at her, but when his eyes met hers she knew that he wasn't seeing any of the bitter fury she was feeling. He was barely even seeing her; his mind was still on Greenbriar.

"Lane, if you'll just give me a few minutes . . ." he began.

"Forget it," she snapped. "I know now that your priorities haven't changed one bit since the minute you came here and I never should have expected that they would."

She held his eyes, willing him to recognize her feelings; then she spoke again quickly, terrified that he would see them and simply ignore them. "So I won't ask for any of your precious time—today or later. I won't ask for anything from you except to be left alone."

She turned abruptly and almost ran out of the house and down the path, throwing herself into the refuge of her jeep. She sat gripping the wheel for a minute while she blinked away the tears that were blurring her vision, then, with a vicious gesture, she turned the key in the ignition and gunned the motor.

A cold hollow place was forming inside her and steadily growing bigger. All she could think about was getting as far away from Vance as possible, as if putting distance between them could make that void go away.

She backed out into the turnaround, spraying gravel out into the trees, then drove dangerously fast down the drive and even after she was out on the highway. In only a few minutes she was several miles away from the house on the lake, but the empty feeling was still with her.

And so was the answer she'd gone there for: The real Vance was the man who had made her so furious the day she'd learned his identity. He was not the man who'd made love to her the day before.

Thad was whistling softly between his teeth as he sat on his heels in the back of his pickup truck, unwrapping dulcimers and taking them out of the large wooden crate one by one. He was handing each one to Lane, and she was setting them carefully on the short counter he had just constructed at right angles to the truck out of some wooden crates and boards.

It seemed to Lane that he was an example of perfect contentment. He's enough to make everyone at the crafts fair start whistling, too, she thought with a wry smile. Everybody but me.

She finished laying out the finished instruments on the quilt he'd spread over the rough boards and stood for a minute watching the last of the mist burn off in the valley. Vehicles of all descriptions were beginning to find their way into the wide hollow that everyone still called Bittercreek Mill, although the mill hadn't been in operation for years. She wondered whether Vance would be one of the hundreds of people who would come to the crafts fair before the day was over.

Probably not, she decided. He'd know that she would be there. Over the past few days he seemed to have been avoiding her just as carefully as she'd been avoiding him. With a sigh she turned back to see what else she could do to help Thad. She might not feel like whistling, but at least she wasn't crying, she thought wryly. Progress was progress.

"I'm going to set up my workbench right here on this table," Thad told her as he swiftly unfolded a sturdy card table and set it up by his makeshift counter. "Last year lots of people came around just to watch and ask questions about how I make the dulcimers, and quite a few of them ended up buying one of the finished ones I had or ordering a special one of their own."

Within an hour or so Thad's workbench had proven to be just as popular as it had been the previous year, and a group of ten or so people were standing around it watching him as he began to carve the sound holes in the top of the instrument he was making out of his favorite cherry wood.

One old man nodded approval at Thad's choice of tools. "Cain't beat a good pocketknife fer that," he announced. "Nor for a lot of other things. Never did see no sense in all them fancy carvin' tools." He squinted at the work. "But that don't look like no heart you're a'carvin'," he objected.

"Dulcimores is supposed to have hearts in the top."

His wife smiled at Lane, the wrinkles around her narrow blue eyes deepening. "Ain't that the way of a man?" she asked. "So old-timey and stuck in a rut a person can't do nothin' new."

Lane laughed with her. "They can be difficult sometimes," she agreed.

At the sound of her laugh the old man's attention turned to her. "Say, howdy there. Ain't you the gal that was writin' down all the old stories? Did you git mine all wrote down that I told you about the mines?"

She looked at him intently, and then she realized that he was the old coal miner who had button-holed her on the main street of Covey the after-noon she had been trying to get ready for that very first meeting with Vance.

"Why, hello, Mr. Cotton." She held out her hand in greeting. "I've been intending to come and see you. We never did get to finish our conversation that day."

"Wal, I've got lots more to tell ye. . . ." He looked as if he were about to start telling her right then, but he was interrupted by a shrill young voice.

"Don't tell her another thing, Uncle Jasper."

The voice was loud, and there was such a note of purposeful intensity in it that everyone within reach turned to look for the source. Lane looked for it, too, even though she knew whose voice it was. Sure enough, Rowena and Janie were joining their group.

"She's gonna make a lot of money off of you if you let her," Rowena went on, her green eyes as indignant as her voice. "She's not writing anything down for a university—she's working for that Morgan guy at Greenbriar Park. The two of 'em are gonna make television commercials out of us!"

Rowena had the complete attention of everyone near Thad's workbench now, and people were starting to drift over from all directions as they sensed a scene unfolding. Lane just stood, dumbfounded, her hand on the back of the folding chair she'd been using.

Rowena looked around, her face glowing with satisfaction at the number of people now hanging onto her next pronouncement. Janie stood beside her, a self-righteous smile on her face as she nodded agreement.

"She pretends to be real friendly and then, when she's alone with *Mr.* Morgan, she says we're 'different' and 'colorful,'" Rowena continued, the words rolling out, almost as if she couldn't stop them.

She flashed a glance at Lane, that horrible, resentful look that had become so familiar to her; then she looked at Thad, directing her next words to him. "She's making fools out of all of us," she declared.

Lane's mind was racing. Why was Rowena saying those things? What on earth was she talking about?

"You've all seen her with him. They've been going around everywhere together; she's been introducing him to everyone. They're working together to make money off of us and take advantage of us just like the outsiders have always done."

Rowena paused to let the whole idea sink in. It flashed through Lane's consciousness that *this* was at the root of all those horrid, hateful looks she'd gotten from her, that Rowena had been holding all this resentment and anger inside for weeks and now it was all pouring out.

She'd wanted to know what was wrong between them, she thought quickly, wildly, but she certainly hadn't expected to find out in front of half the people in the county.

She tried to defend herself. "But, Rowena . . ."

Rowena ignored her. She was rolling and she wasn't about to be stopped.

"And do you know what *Mr. Morgan* says about us when he thinks no one but Lane is listening? He says we're 'curious,' and that the whole world ought to come and see us!" she finished triumphantly, as if that alone were enough to prove beyond all doubt that she was right.

By now Lane couldn't talk at all. This attack was so unexpected, so insane, so groundless, that she couldn't think of a single word to say. She stood still in her tracks, as if she were rooted to the ground, staring at the girl, trying to look into her eyes, trying to understand how she had come to this conclusion.

Then it hit her. That afternoon on the porch! That golden afternoon she had spent with Vance! She had been right when she thought she had seen Rowena just inside the window.

The girl must have been listening to them, picking up certain words and phrases, hearing but not understanding what they were saying. She had just fastened on to the few things she had picked up and drawn the conclusion that Lane was a complete hypocrite and a liar.

No wonder Rowena had stopped speaking to her! If she thought that Lane was working for

Vance for profit, and not for the university, then she thought that Lane had betrayed her friendship. Hers, and that of every other inhabitant of the mountains! That explained everything.

Lane's voice broke into the stillness that had fallen when Rowena stopped speaking. "Rowena, you've misunderstood. I was friends with Vance Morgan, and I introduced him to some people, but I don't work for him. I never have."

So many eyes were on her, she thought, and none of them were very friendly. Her own gaze moved from Rowena to the others in the group. Suddenly she felt terribly exposed and vulnerable.

She began to search the faces turned to her for signs that nothing had changed, that she was still accepted, that nobody believed the wild things Rowena had just said.

Many of these people she didn't know; *they* would probably tend to believe Rowena. She looked to Jasper Cotton and his cheerful little wife. They were looking back at her curiously, worriedly, but stronger than those emotions was the hard suspicion that was forming on their faces.

She turned to Thad. Surely he knew her well enough to know that the charges were totally preposterous. "Thad, you know that . . ."

But he didn't even let her finish the sentence. He met her eyes for the briefest moment, then turned to the people gathered in front of his workbench. His cheerfully brittle tones cut through the hum of voices that had begun, the haze of muttered comments and speculations that was beginning to swirl around Lane's ears.

"Now come on, folks," he said. "We're supposed to be talking about dulcimers here, and we've gotta decide if Jasper is right. Do they all have to have hearts in the top?"

There was a tension underlying the casualness of his tone, and Lane knew from the brief glance that he'd given her that he was not at all sure what to believe. He was giving serious consideration to Rowena's accusations.

A terrible, sick feeling invaded her stomach. Of course he would believe them, and so would everyone else. A story like that made perfect sense to these people—it was the continuing story of their lives and the lives of at least two generations before them.

People had been coming in from the outside for a long time and exploiting them, robbing them of timber and coal and water power, and giving them practically nothing in return. Thad and Jasper Cotton and his wife and all the others would reason the same way Rowena had done: Why should it be any different now? Why shouldn't these strangers be here to exploit their identities for the sake of a lot of money?

The sickness that had begun in her stomach spread to her limbs. She reached under the counter for her purse and slid its thin strap onto her shoulder. She looked at the group in front of her, but they were a blur—she couldn't see a single individual, not even Rowena.

"I just want you to know that I haven't lied to you," she said suddenly, clearly, almost before she knew that she was going to speak. "Rowena overheard part of a conversation and she misunderstood it. Please remember that."

She walked away then, her only thought to go

and find Alice. Alice would be the only one who would believe her.

The next few days were a study in human nature, she thought later. But at the time she was too vulnerable, too sensitive, too hurt and worried, to be that objective. She wasn't thinking about human nature—she was just trying to survive.

Alice did believe her, and she was Lane's staunchest defender. Other people, some of whom really surprised Lane, defended her, too. But most of her defenders were the people who knew her best, the ones whom she had already taped and interviewed.

She began to feel almost panicky. All her securities were slipping away from her; first the brief feeling of unfathomable security that she'd found in Vance's arms, and now the welcome that she'd always received in the mountains. And that could lead to the loss of the one thing she'd always depended on—her work.

If she were going to finish everything Dr. Burroughs wanted before the time period allotted to her grant ran out, she would have to spend a lot of time with some people who she *didn't* know very well. And many of those were the ones who had accepted Rowena's charges against her without question. Now it took every ounce of nerve she had simply to approach somebody new.

She tried to push that thought away as she walked rapidly down the main street of Covey. The summer air was hot and close and it dragged at her. She had to walk fast or she would sit down under a tree and never move again.

She had to start thinking positively and assume that she would get a good reaction from people, or she might as well quit now, she lectured herself. She couldn't let this stop her.

She looked for traffic in the narrow street, then crossed it to walk the last block to Mattie's. She was going to go in there for lunch no matter how uncomfortable it might be. She grinned wryly as she heard those words ringing in her head, first in Alice's voice, then in Granny Belle's.

They had both told her over and over again that there was nothing she could do except carry on with her life as usual and let people learn for themselves that she had been telling the truth. Granny had even ridden the bus up from Cedar Creek to alternately lecture and comfort Lane after she had called. She had said that it was time that she came to "see about" Lane, that she always went somewhere in the summer and that she liked to ride the bus and never did get to much, but Lane had known the truth: Granny had come because of the way Lane had sounded when she'd made her weekly phone call after she'd come home from the crafts fair at Bittercreek Mill.

Well, she wasn't going to let Granny or Alice or herself down, she thought as she continued to walk quickly along the street. People were ultimately fair minded, and when they had time to think about things they'd realize that Rowena was wrong.

Just before she reached Mattie's, though, her steps slowed and she tried frantically to think of a reason not to go in. She lingered for a minute outside, looking into the window of the dress shop next door, not really seeing the uninteresting slacks and blouse on the slightly shopworn mannequin that was its only inhabitant.

Finally, with a sigh, she turned and reached for the handle of the door to the café.

It moved in her hand, and she looked up quickly. Vance's strongly chiseled face was within inches of her own. His brown eyes were gazing at her keenly.

"I've been watching you for more than a minute," he told her, his low voice as intimate as it had been by the waterfall. "And I just can't believe you'd be that engrossed in this." His other hand dismissed the outfit. "It's not your style, you know."

Suddenly she wanted to weep. She just wanted to lean forward across the short distance between them, lay her head on his massive chest and simply cry her eyes out. He was so close, and she could smell his wonderful, masculine scent; he was so warm and his arms were a sheltering haven. She was exhausted and scared and she needed him.

Her eyes clung to his then, without conscious thought, moved to caress his face and roam over his sensual lips.

She felt tears begin to crowd beneath her lids. They stood on her lower lashes, but she didn't brush them away. She couldn't; she couldn't move at all. She had to stay exactly where she was or she would go into his arms.

"Lane, what *are* you doing standing out here on the sidewalk?" he asked. He raised his hand to her face, cupping her cheek lightly and running the side of his thumb along her cheekbone.

The sensation of his skin against hers reached into her, called to her very soul. It called back the memories of the times when he had held her in his arms, and it terrified her. She couldn't stand this— it would be a heavenly comfort to go into his arms, but she wouldn't be able to take it when she was wrenched out of them again. She wasn't strong enough for that now.

"I'm going into the café," she said, almost in a whisper. It was taking every ounce of strength she had just to think about moving away from him; she didn't have any energy left for her voice.

"I'll go back in with you," he offered. "I've been wanting to talk with you." His eyes bored into hers. "Lane, why haven't you returned my calls?"

She could answer him. She could tell him why she hadn't called him back, and they could talk about the last time they'd met.

But it would do no good, her mind cried silently as her eyes searched his. We could talk all day and we'd still be the same two people we are now. We'll never change enough to be together forever, and I can't live with anything else.

She shook her head. "That would be even worse," she said disjointedly. "It's hard enough for me to go in there alone."

"Lane, will you try to make sense? What are you talking about?"

"About the fact that everybody thinks I'm working for you instead of for the university. About the fact that my work is at a standstill."

All the misery of the last few days came over her again, and she stepped away from him and into the doorway.

"That's ridiculous," he said sharply. "Gloria hasn't bothered you again, and one incident isn't going to bring your work to a standstill."

His tone, his sudden change from tenderness to impatience, slashed her fragile emotions. It fragmented them and swirled the pieces into an incoherent mixture. The old anger came to the top.

"I think I'm the best judge of that." Her voice was trembling just as her hands were. "My work is probably the one area of my life where I know what I'm doing, and I certainly think that I can judge its progress or lack thereof."

His eyes held hers, the puzzled concern and frustration in them pulling her, trying to draw an explanation out of her. She had to get away.

"Look, Vance." Her words were abrupt, almost harsh. "I have to be going now. Good-bye."

She turned her back to him and went into the noisy little restaurant.

Chapter Ten

$\mathcal{L}$ane was winding her hair into a smooth chignon low on the back of her neck when Alice knocked lightly at the open door.

"Can I come in and collapse for a minute? I'm worn out just from trying to keep my mouth shut."

Lane laughed. "I know, Alice. That's one of the hardest things anybody can do." She inserted the last long, golden hairpin and turned from the mirror to smile at the older woman. "However, you're doing a beautiful job of it, and I want to congratulate you."

Alice smiled wearily in return. "I guess so. I even talked to Thad a minute when he came to pick Rowena up, and I managed to be almost friendly." She dropped into the old gooseneck rocker that sat between the door and the tall, narrow window. "It's taking all the strength I've got, but I know I don't have a choice. You've helped me see that."

Lane nodded as she came to stand in front of the window for a minute. She lifted her face to the breeze that was springing up, loving the coolness of it after the sultry heat that had enclosed her all day.

"Alice, I think you'll like Thad when you get to know him. One of the things that hurts me the most about all this furor Rowena has stirred up is that it seems to have ruined my relationship with him." She held the thin curtain back and a gust of cooler air came in. "I just can't stand it that he thinks I'm so dishonest; after all, we were really good friends." She turned away from Alice and frowned thoughtfully out into the darkening afternoon.

"Now, honey, I've told you over and over that he'll come around," Alice replied. "And he will, as time goes on. Right now he and Rowena are just scared you've made fools out of them, but they'll soon see different."

"Oh, Alice, I hope so. I'm glad they're getting together, but it makes me sick that it had to be this suspicion of me that did it. It makes me feel really lonesome to lose them both."

"You haven't lost either one of them for good," the older woman reassured her. She reached around Lane to take a magazine from the bedside table and absently began to fan herself with it. "And I'll accept Thad if it keeps me from losing Rowena for good. But I tell you, Lane, every time I watch her leave the house with him I see me and Jason all over again, and my heart just breaks."

"Alice, he isn't Jason," Lane said gently for the thousandth time. "I really think Thad's a good man, and I don't think he'll hurt Rowena."

"Well, maybe not on purpose," Alice said.

"Looking back from this many years I doubt if Jason set out to hurt me, either. But things just happen. Things can happen to any bond—lovers or friends or even relatives."

Lane nodded, and her thoughts flashed to Vance. She walked back to the mirror and picked up her lipstick, then put it down again and moved restlessly toward the armoire, trying to shake off the memory of his rugged face so close to hers. Something had happened to *that* bond, all right. It had been doomed from the beginning.

She took out the simple mauve-colored dress that was her favorite and spread it on the bed while she looked for the high-heeled sandals that matched it.

"But that's just part of living," she said thoughtfully, as much to herself as to Alice. "You can't protect Rowena from that forever."

Alice's silence communicated her agreement; then she stared out into the dusky evening as Lane slipped into the dress and buttoned the narrow straps at each shoulder. When Alice returned her attention to the room she inspected Lane, then gave her an approving smile.

"You look like you're the one who's gonna need some protection," she said, "'cause that's a dress to wear to meet a brown-eyed, handsome man."

The words from the traditional mountain song cut into Lane. They were an uncannily accurate description of Vance and they opened the corner of her heart where she'd been holding her memories of him. She looked at her reflection, letting the memories of him wash over her, wondering for a minute how she would look to him.

The dress fit her to perfection. Its lines were

clean and classic, falling from the shoulders, where the tiny straps and buttons formed its only ornaments. The soft silk molded itself over her high, firm breasts and clung to the long curves of her thighs. Its color, a mixture of blue, gray and lilac, was perfect for her; it set off the golden tones of her hair and picked up all the variable shades in her eyes.

Vance *would* like it, she thought, and with that thought came another: It didn't make any difference. He would never see her in it.

"I wish I *were* meeting a brown-eyed, handsome man tonight," she said, forcing a lightness she didn't feel into her tone. "But I'm meeting Judge Slone and his wife instead." She sat down to fasten the thin straps of her sandals. "At least, I think I am. We planned all this before Rowena's big announcement, and when I tried to call this afternoon to confirm the appointment I got no answer."

She finished with the last tiny buckle and rose quickly, rummaging in the chest of drawers for her slim straw purse. "Judge Slone is supposed to tell me all about the old courthouse, and Mrs. Slone wants to share some anecdotes about her grandfather, who was the first lawyer in the county."

Alice nodded, hardly hearing what Lane was telling her. "Well, drive carefully," she said as Lane finished transferring her essentials to the little purse and picked up a light wrap. "It's cooling off, so it may be pretty foggy later on."

Alice was right. The fog was beginning to form in isolated spots even before Lane reached The Woodfern, its gray and white tendrils swirling against the darkening evening and obscuring the edges of the road in places. She was glad to drive through the last patch of it as she turned the jeep into the resort's driveway and drove up the hill to the restaurant's parking lot.

She pulled the wispy purple mohair stole around her shoulders as she climbed the stone steps; the air was definitely getting cooler. But there was another reason why she needed to feel something warm around her, she admitted to herself as her eyes roamed over the flowering bushes and trees beside the path.

The last time she'd been there Vance had been with her, his hand on her arm warming her entire body, his lips on hers. Just being there brought it all back—that day, the day in his arms by the waterfall and every other time she'd ever seen him. It brought back the taste of his skin on her tongue, the feel of his hard length pressing against her body, the hot, tingling excitement of his mouth on her breast.

She tried to shake off the memories, but they had just been waiting to capture her again, and by the time she found herself facing the maître d' she could hardly realize that she wasn't there to meet Vance this time.

"I . . . I'm meeting Judge and Mrs. Slone," she stammered.

"This way, please, the table is reserved."

He led her to a table near the doors that led out to the terrace. She ordered a glass of white wine from the waiter who had followed them, then settled back into the deep chair. Thick, dark blue drapes were closed over the french doors, and the dark wood of the room combined with the dim lighting to make this a different place from the sunny patio where she'd been with Vance. Nevertheless, her thoughts clung to him.

The waiter brought the wine, and she sipped it, enjoying the fruity aroma. She tried to relax, but the tension that had become her constant companion was beginning to build again and she wished that she could leave. Maybe if she could get away from these reminders of Vance her disquiet would lessen.

Restlessly she glanced at her watch. It was past the time when she was supposed to meet the Slones, almost fifteen minutes past. She glanced toward the door again, hoping to see them arriving.

Her breath caught in her throat, along with a swallow of wine, and she brought her large white napkin to her mouth. Instead of the portly figures of the judge and his wife, Vance's tall, lean body was outlined against the door.

The shiny tracery of the baroque design etched in the frosted glass formed a contrasting background for the clean lines of his dark head and broad shoulders. He was dressed as if for a business appointment in a three-piece suit of a rich caramel color and a pale beige shirt. She drank in every detail hungrily, instinctively wanting to go to him, to touch him.

He felt her eyes on him and turned. Involuntarily he moved in her direction, and at first she thought he was going to approach her table. Even from across the large room she could feel the intensity of his gaze that had drawn her to him the day they met, and her heart thudded painfully.

She didn't want to see him; she didn't want to talk to him and be torn apart all over again. She didn't want his tender concern first and then his impatient preoccupation with his business the way he'd been in the past.

But she couldn't tell her body that. Her eyes held him, clinging to him against her wishes, as if they could will him to come to her. She tore them away and quickly lowered her head to take another sip of wine. This was all she needed! His memory alone was too much for her to handle on top of the crisis in her work, and now there he was in the flesh!

When she looked up again, though, he was following the maître d' toward the separate room that held the bar.

Disappointment stabbed her. He wasn't even going to speak to her because she had walked away from him at Mattie's. She had in essence told him to mind his own business, and evidently that was what he intended to do.

Impulsively she reached for her purse. All she wanted was to get out of there, to get as far away from him as possible. The Slones probably weren't coming anyway.

The waiter's voice at her elbow stopped her. "Miss Matthews? You have a telephone call. Would you come this way, please?"

She followed him through the door of the small office discreetly hidden behind the tall plants clustered in the foyer. Judge Slone's voice crackled over the wire.

"Miss Matthews? We're so sorry, but we won't be able to keep our appointment." His voice faded, then became stronger again. "We got as far as Caney Crossing, but then we had to turn around and come back home. The fog, you know. Mrs. Slone just refuses to stay out in it."

Lane assured him that she understood and agreed that they would make another appointment when they had a better connection. She hung up the phone, wondering whether the judge had given her his real reason for not coming to The Woodfern.

It was hard to believe that the fog had gotten so much worse already, but the Slones lived several miles away from The Woodfern in the opposite direction from Covey, so maybe it was thicker over there. On the other hand, maybe they'd heard the rumors about her supposed deception and, no matter what they believed, were staying away from the controversy.

She opened the door of the office and stepped out, still thinking about the Slones.

"Lane!" a deep voice greeted her and turned her legs to liquid. "I'd like you to meet someone."

Vance was in the doorway of the bar, apparently saying good-bye to a business associate. Her heart lurched at the sight of him, and she wished fervently that she'd been able to leave without seeing him again. He was so handsome and so desirable that it hurt.

There was no way to escape, though; she would have to talk to him, to stand near him, no matter how much it upset her. She joined them and was introduced to the man, who greeted her politely and then left almost immediately.

"What reason could you possibly have had for wanting me to meet him?" she demanded as soon as the door had closed. "I can't imagine what connection I have with a man who sells equipment for parks."

"You don't," he answered with a teasing grin,

taking her arm and walking her back into the dining room as he spoke. "I wanted to talk to you and I thought you might not turn your back and leave me if I had a witness."

"Vance, you make me sound so *rude.*"

"You'll have to admit that you weren't too polite yesterday at the café."

On the surface his tone was light, but there was an undertone of seriousness in it that angered her. The nerve of him! He was acting as if she had slapped his face for no reason at all.

"Well, *you'll* have to admit that you weren't exactly cordial the last time I came to your office," she retorted as they reached her table. "As I recall, you didn't have five minutes for me."

She wanted to add, "And that was after we'd had a day together that should have given us an eternity for each other," but her pride stopped her. If he could forget that day at the waterfall so completely, so could she.

He stopped behind the chair where she'd been sitting and pulled it out for her. "That's one of the things I want to talk to you about," he said smoothly. "We can discuss it over dinner."

She continued to stand. "But I don't intend to stay. I was supposed to meet some people, but they aren't coming."

"Great. I was meeting someone, too, but I got rid of him as soon as I saw that you were here. I want to get things straightened out between us." He held the chair out with such confident authority that, without any conscious volition, she moved closer to him and sat down.

He went around the table and sat down opposite her, signaling to the waiter as he did so. Her hands were trembling with anger and apprehension, and she just nodded curtly when he offered to order something for her. She certainly couldn't think about food right then.

How had she gotten into this? True, she wanted to tell him exactly what she thought about the way he'd responded to the problem with Gloria and Polly Clay, how she had felt so terribly betrayed, but she didn't want to do it over dinner.

How could she? How could she spend the evening with him when it was so apparent that he just wanted to talk her out of being angry so he wouldn't feel guilty anymore? All he wanted was to get their relationship back on a civilized basis.

And all she wanted was . . . She watched the play of candlelight on the chiseled planes of his face as he looked at the wine list. She watched the curve of his lips as he spoke to the waiter and she admitted the truth. All she wanted was to go back into his arms as she had that day by the waterfall and stay there forever.

Stung by the admission, the insanity of that desire after the way he had treated her, she leaned back and toyed with the edge of her napkin, forcing her eyes to stay away from him. She would just get through this quickly, she thought, and then they'd part for good. She was too vulnerable, too insecure about everything in her life, to cope with him.

"I've been trying to apologize ever since that day you came to my office," Vance said as the waiter poured the wine that he had selected. "I didn't mean to be abrupt with you, but I was totally immersed in that ad campaign, and it *was* urgent."

"Well, my problem was urgent, too. If Gloria had kept following me around she would have ruined every contact I had." She sipped her wine, thinking how absurd that fear of Gloria's behavior was now in light of all that had happened since. "But it turns out that I bothered you for nothing—Rowena managed to destroy my work with no help at all from Gloria."

"Rowena? I thought she was your friend."

He was leaning toward her, truly interested, listening carefully for her reply. She felt herself begin to relax. Suddenly it felt so good to be talking to him again—to be able to tell him about the nightmare of the last few days.

"She's been pretty distant for quite a while," Lane began as the waiter returned with their appetizers. "It all started when Thad was going around with me and introducing me to people. She's had a crush on him forever, and she thought I was taking him away from her."

She paused to take a spoonful of the thick homemade tomato soup, then looked up into his eyes again. "Vance, do you remember the afternoon when we took Old Man to the church at Chalky Mountain?"

The darkness of his eyes picked up the gleam from the candle, and he smiled. He nodded, his eyes never leaving hers.

"Remember later when we were sitting on the porch and I thought I saw Rowena just inside the window?"

"Yes," he said quickly, almost abruptly, as if he were impatient for her to go on. He was listening with his whole body the way he did sometimes—concentrating every ounce of his being on her and her thoughts and feelings. He was with her in a way no one else ever was; they were friends once more.

So she told him the entire story while they finished the soup and ate the fresh baby trout, faintly smoked and garnished with a subtly spicy cream sauce.

"Vance, she made me feel that this was seventeenth-century Salem, and I was being declared a witch," she concluded. "It's been horrible." To her dismay, her voice almost broke.

"I'm sorry," he said, his rich voice an incredible comfort. "I'm so sorry you've had to go through all this. But it'll soon be over. People will see that she's wrong about you."

All during the meal the old feeling of closeness had been coming back again, stronger than it had ever been between them, and now it combined with the tenderness in his voice to shatter the few remnants of control that she had left.

The desire to go to him that had seized her on the street the day before flooded over her again and instinctively she reached out to him. It wasn't something to think about; it was simply wrong for them to be this close and not to touch.

His big hand closed over her smaller one, then turned it over, his thumb drawing sensual circles on her sensitive palm as his eyes burned into hers. She couldn't move; she could no longer breathe—her hand felt as if he were tracing that design into it with molten metal, and an answering heat was beginning to rise in her.

He took a last sip of wine from the glass he held in his other hand, then he set it down very carefully, his strong brown fingers handling the fragile stem of the glass with easy grace.

"Lane, come with me," he said. "Don't say a word, just come with me."

He walked very close by her side across the big, dimly lit room, but they didn't touch again until they stepped out into the moist foggy night.

The fog had moved in to fill the entire valley below The Woodfern, and it created a thick white world that swallowed them up as soon as they were outside the door. Vance put his arm around her then, and she moved against him, thrilling to the touch of the length of him against her.

The opalescent mist was everywhere, but he walked quickly and confidently across the lawn, finding the path that led up and away from the restaurant. She knew that they'd passed the steps that led down to the parking lot; she knew that they were moving up and into the trees. She couldn't see where they were going, but she didn't care.

He was holding her very close against him as they walked, and all she could think about was the touch of his thigh against hers, the feel of his muscular arm around her back and the touch of his hand just under her breast. They blotted out her consciousness of the rest of the world as effectively as the rolling gray haze obscured the sight of it. She was with Vance, and nothing else mattered.

They moved up onto flat stepping-stones and crossed a stone-paved terrace to arrive at the door of one of the guest houses that were scattered through the trees on the hillside. He inserted his key, and they stepped inside. A lamp was burning at one end of the deep couch, and in its low light Lane got an impression of a spacious suite of rooms that seemed to echo the natural charm of their woodsy setting.

As soon as the door was closed behind them, he

stepped away from her, and she was filled with a terrible sense of loss.

"Don't move," he murmured huskily. "Stay just where you are."

He removed his coat and vest and dropped them on the couch, then went toward the mantel. She was dimly aware that he took something from it; then she heard him moving around in another room and the sounds of doors opening and closing. She couldn't think enough to even care what he was doing; all she wanted was for him to come back to her, to touch her again, to hold her against his warm body.

He came back into the room, but only to cross the corner of it and disappear again. His eyes sought hers in a quick, burning glance, but he said nothing. It seemed like an eternity, but she didn't move from the spot where he had left her. She couldn't break the spell.

At last he was beside her. "Come on now," he whispered. "Come with me."

She walked in the circle of his arm into the bedroom and stopped just inside the doorway. She gasped, her breath drawn from her by what she saw. All around the room, on the tables beside the bed, on the diagonal mantel in the corner, on the window ledges, and even on the floor, were candles, their flickering light filling the room with a yellow glow.

He stepped away from her slightly and turned to take her shoulders gently in his hands.

"I just had to see you in the candlelight," he told her softly. "I had to."

He kissed her once, very gently, his lips brushing

hers like a dream. But still he held his body away
from hers, their only connection his hands on her
shoulders. Then his fingers moved to the buttons
on her dress and deftly slipped them through to let
it fall down around her into a soft pool at her feet.

She stood in the lacy, lilac-colored strapless
teddy that was holding up her silky hose and looked
for a long time into his eyes. Then, very deliberately, she stepped out of first one and then the other of
her high-heeled sandals, and her own hands moved
to loosen his tie and undo the buttons of his shirt.

He shrugged his shirt off while his eyes devoured
her. She loved watching as their dark depths caressed the slender length of her smooth legs, the
flatness of her stomach, the smallness of her waist
and then the high fullness of her breasts, trembling
under the thin fabric that covered them. Her
nipples were hard now with hunger and they were
thrusting toward him in a shameless invitation for
his caress.

His eyes clung to them, and he reached out to
circle each of them in turn with one long finger;
then he bent and kissed one, then the other, lightly
at first, then hungrily. His lips and his tongue
pulled at them through the gossamer cloth, and she
gasped with delight, moaning a little and winding
her hands into his hair.

In one sweeping movement he raised his head to
gaze into her face, and the dark pools of his eyes
awoke a melting desire in her that traveled into
every corner of her being. He whisked the garment
away from the ivory mounds it covered, then bent
his head again to taste their sweetness without any
obstruction.

The thrill of his warm, moist lips and tongue on

her swollen nipples shot through her like a flame, and she reached for the buckle on his belt, unfastening it with one hand as she held his head to her with the other.

"Vance, I've needed you so. . . ." She heard her ragged whisper before she even knew she was going to speak. "Vance . . ."

His lips found hers in answer, and his tongue outlined them, tasting them briefly. Then his mouth crushed hers with a passion that was almost out of control. Her mouth fell open, and her tongue came to meet his, to welcome it and tell him again what she had just put into words.

He took her into that whirlpool of ecstasy that she had remembered a dozen times since that day on the mountain, and this time it was even wilder and more enticing than it had been before. His mouth and his hands knew her body now; they knew how to please her, to tease her, to drive her almost to distraction.

His hands roamed over her back, over the curves of her hips, searching and taking as if he could never get enough of the feel of her. That delicious friction called to her very soul, and every particle of her body was exploding with wanting him.

He broke the kiss at last and pulled away to quickly remove the rest of their clothing. When that was finished he stepped away and let his eyes roam hungrily over every inch of her.

"You are so beautiful," he said slowly, rhythmically, almost as if it were a song. "Your skin glows as if you were a candle yourself."

He reached out to her then and began to pull the pins from her hair, removing them carefully, one by one, as if this were a ritual that he loved. It came loose at last, and its weight tumbled around her shoulders and down her back as he took her hand and led her to the bed.

They lay down together, each of them reluctant to have any space at all between them. She delighted in the feel of his skin against hers, in the weight of his leg across hers, as he stroked her back and held her to him as if he were trying to melt them into one.

His lips found hers again, and their kiss was long and sweet. She was falling again, falling into that marvelous swirl of delectable darkness only he could create for her. His hands stroked over the bend of her waist, her long legs, her hips, and came back to caress the sensitive skin of her inner thighs. Then they slipped into her hair and tangled there, cupping her head and bringing his tongue even deeper into her mouth.

Every touch built the wanting in her. She explored the muscular surface of his broad back, the expanse of his chest, stroking the warm tautness of his skin with her open palm. She moved her legs against his, and when she felt the long strength of his thighs on the inside of hers, she used every inch of her body to communicate the desire that was shaking her to the depths of her being.

When his lips left her mouth and began to trail down her neck with more kisses and tiny nibbles to find her breasts again, she trembled with the marvelous torment and arched against him, calling his name. He teased her hard nipples with his lips and his tongue and his teeth, caressing them until the flashing excitement she felt in them was singing in every one of her veins.

Then she felt him leave her, and she opened her

eyes, moaning a little in protest. But he hadn't gone far. He was kneeling above her, his eyes heavy-lidded with desire, stroking her now with his look as he had been doing with his hands.

She drank in the sight of him, big and incredibly handsome in the flickering light that touched every corner of the room with gold and shadow.

"I used to think you were made of sunshine," he whispered, his voice low and ragged. "But you're also made of candlelight. You're my golden girl."

He bent his head and carefully placed one kiss very low on her flat abdomen. Then he looked up, and his gaze transmitted a fiery current of wanting that blotted out everything in her except her longing for him.

She reached for him with a trembling need that only he could fulfill. She arched into him as he came to her and took him in to share the dizzying passion storming through them both, the wanting and the need in them that could only be met by this joyous unity.

The sweet thrusts built and built until she felt that she was poised on the edge of pure rapture. And then the passion in his body, the aliveness of his hands and the magic of his mouth, pulled her over the precipice, and she fell into a chasm filled with a pleasure so great that she could hardly bear it.

She cried out his name over and over again, and the sound mingled with the richness of his voice as he answered. A golden heat was coursing through her that was more wonderful than all of the candles that surrounded them, and it carried with it a happiness that she thought would break her heart.

Chapter Eleven

Lane floated back to consciousness, stretching luxuriously under the smoothness of the sheets, pulling them up against the still-cool air of the very early morning. Without opening her eyes she burrowed more deeply into the pillow, gradually becoming aware of the contentment that was spreading through her more strongly with every move she made toward waking. There was a happy, sated feeling filling every cell of her body, and sleepily she wondered why. Then she remembered.

Instinctively she reached for Vance. He was beside her, still asleep, his face turned toward the windows that were open now, the drapes pulled back. He must have been up earlier and come back to bed; the room had been a closed, private world the night before.

She lay propped up on one elbow, watching him, loving the contrast of his thick, tousled hair so startlingly black against the pastel pillowcase, loving the clean lines of his profile and the tiny lines around his eyes that showed white in the darkness of his tan. She drank in every detail of his face; then her eyes roamed over the length of him, sprawled so intimately beside her under the sheet.

A wave of feeling like nothing she had ever felt before washed over her, and she trembled with the force of it. She loved him! She loved him and she needed him so. She needed his strength; she needed the warmth of his brown eyes smiling into hers; she needed his body melded into hers. She loved him more than she had ever loved anyone; he was a part of her, and suddenly she felt that she was a different person. There was no way now that she could imagine going on without him beside her.

Her hand shaking with the magnitude of that realization, she brushed back her hair and then reached out to him. She wanted to caress every muscular inch of him, to draw him into her arms and hold him there forever.

His breathing was deep and even though, and his face was so peaceful that she hesitated, caressing him with her eyes. She didn't want to disturb him. Instead she wanted to capture this moment and keep it for the rest of her life so that she would always have this precious time on a sunny morning when she felt so incredibly filled with love.

She watched him for a few minutes longer. Then, unable to resist, she touched him very gently with the tip of her finger, lightly smoothing away the tiny creases in the tanned skin of his face, then tracing the arch of his thick dark brows.

His eyes opened. A smile for her was already in them.

He spent a long minute just looking at her, not saying a word. Then, with a quick, lithe movement, he turned onto his other side and ran his hand under the sheet to follow the curve of her waist and rest possessively on her hip.

The familiarity of the gesture, the comforting closeness of it, made her breath catch in her throat. It seemed to be a sharing, a confirmation of the love she was feeling, and without a conscious thought her arms encircled him.

He kissed her lightly, then held her very close, his cheek against hers. They lay without speaking, just holding each other in an embrace that needed no words, a nearness that made them a part of the forest just outside, a part of the morning itself.

The sound of the insects on the hillside and the lushness of the summer air filled the room.

"I don't think I knew that crickets or locusts or whatever those things are existed until I met you," he murmured, his face hidden in her hair. "And I didn't know that the air could feel like this on a summer morning . . ." He drew away so that he could see her eyes. "Or that a foggy night could be pure magic."

She felt the heat rush into her face at the mention of the night before and, suddenly shy, she lowered her eyes and buried her face in the hollow of his neck.

"Oh, Vance . . ." she breathed, and she had to bite her lip to keep the rest of the words inside. Every fiber of her wanted to say, "And *I* never knew what it was like to be in love until I met you," but her pride wouldn't let her.

Memories of the night before washed over her. Every kiss, every touch, every word he had said

came spinning through her mind. He had told her
how beautiful she was and how desirable; he had
murmured that her skin glowed like the candles he
had lit for her, but he had never said the word
"love" at all.

She had ached to hear him say that he loved her
before she'd fallen asleep in his arms, and this
morning it was a desperate desire. She wound her
arms more tightly around him and ran her hands
across his muscular shoulders in a caress that
begged him to say it, but he only held her more
tightly and began to nibble at her earlobe.

He trailed a path of tiny kisses down the side of
her neck, and when he continued it across her bare
shoulder and down her arm to bury his lips in her
palm she began to forget that there was something
she wanted him to say. All she could think about
was what she wanted him to do, and with a
trembling sigh she twined her fingers in his hair and
brought his lips to hers.

Her mouth was open beneath his, and when his
tongue touched hers, she encircled it with her lips
and caressed it with her own. She tried to draw
enough of the honey from it to make up for all the
time before she'd known him; how could she
possibly have existed for all those years?

His hand drew circles on her back while they
kissed, winding around and around in a pattern
that stoked the flame that was rising in her. It was
setting her skin afire in every place it touched, and
she moaned softly, moving even closer to him,
pressing her lips to his until they melted together.

He cupped her shoulder and caressed it with one
big hand, and the burning circles he traced there
pulled her back into the swirling maelstrom of

passion that only he could create. The sound of the
birds and insects outside became louder, the fresh
forest smells became sharper, more sensual, then
they faded as his lips bruised hers, as if they all had
been created only as a backdrop for his touch.

His strong hand found her breast confidently,
surely, and cupped its heavy fullness. He caressed
the nipple between his thumb and finger until she
moaned against his lips with the pleasure of it and
with the pain of wanting still more. Her hands
pressed against his head to bring his mouth even
closer to hers, then traveled down the sides of his
strong neck to caress the width of his shoulders and
pull them toward her, as if she would gather all of
him into her arms if she could.

Her hands explored his body hungrily; the palms
of her hands seemed to become almost a part of his
skin. She was trying to draw the essence of him
in through her pores, trying to memorize with
her touch the muscular beauty of his shoulders,
the length of his back, the curves of his slim
hips.

Finally he broke the kiss and replaced it with
several light, urgent ones scattered over her face
and throat. She kissed him back, raining rapid little
kisses onto the hard planes of his face in answer,
playing with him, telling him her feelings in a new
way, communicating with him as if they had just
discovered a new language all their own.

She ran her fingers lightly down his back and
over his hips again, and his face moved away from
hers. His mouth traced its way down the curve of
her throat and then, without warning, it took the
place of his hand at her breasts. His lips outlined
first one tingling nipple, then the other.

"Vance."

Her voice was the merest whisper, but its tone was as clear as if she had shouted the word. She was making a declaration, a statement that was being torn from her by the force of the emotions that were shaking her. He didn't answer. He didn't seem to hear.

His tongue teased first one and then the other of her small, hard nipples into a peak of desire, and she trembled with the ecstasy. She wanted to tell him that, to make him know the miraculous feelings that were coursing through her, but she didn't know how to put her exultant happiness into words.

His hands caressed her hips, her long legs, the sensitive skin of her inner thighs.

"Vance," she whispered again. "Vance . . ." But she couldn't go on. In the space of only a second she forgot what she had been trying to say. The myriad sensual impressions he was bringing to life for her were destroying her ability to speak, to think.

And then when his mouth left her breasts and began to follow the path that his hands had made over her body he destroyed her ability to move. With a shuddering sigh her hands fell away from him and she lay back, sinking into the softness of the bed as if it were a haven of pure bliss.

She lay without moving for an endless time, experiencing an eternity of pleasurable sensations that left her aware only of his hands, his mouth, his nearness. Then, in spite of her languor, she began to touch him again, very lightly, here and there. She was afraid of distracting him, of stopping him in his wandering, of extinguishing the exquisite sparks of pleasure that sprang into being in every spot where his lips touched her body, but she couldn't help herself.

The tension tore her apart. She didn't want him to stop, but she couldn't keep her hands away from him. At last she ran them into his hair and reveled in its feel against her skin, the crisp strength of it between her fingers. Gradually they cupped around his head and began gently to guide him, to direct him in thrilling and tantalizing her, to lead him to every one of the places that gave her such perfect pleasure.

He followed her guidance with passion, a passion of giving and taking fulfillment that surged between them. She floated in the world of sensation, the world that he was making just for her, and her only consciousness was of the jubilant excitement joining his body and hers.

Then his mouth came back to hers, and she felt the sweet heaviness of his lean length on top of her. She took him in as if she would never let him go, and they moved even deeper into their own private world. Together they began to build again to the incredible exhilaration that they'd shared the night before.

The feelings that filled her were so strong, so much a part of her, that the confession of love she wanted to make surged to her lips again. She held back the words, but she told him how deeply she felt with every touch, every movement of her body with his. She wanted nothing but to hear him say that he loved her; she longed with every ounce of her being to hear him say that they would have this happiness forever, but he didn't. Instead, as they reached the peak of their rapture, he took her face between his hands and cried out just her name.

Afterward they lay for a long time, languidly entangled in the silkiness of the sheets, talking very little. His fingers twined themselves in and out of her hair, and she lay with her face in his shoulder, trying not to think at all.

The morning was moving toward noon, and the air was taking on the sultry quality that it had in the middle of summer when breezes couldn't seem to find their way in between the hills. Somehow the heat that was building in the heavy air began to seep into Lane, to form her disquiet into conscious thoughts again.

Restlessly she ran one hand over the broad expanse of Vance's chest, questioning him without words. After what they had just shared she couldn't envision leaving his arms, much less his life, but she had no idea whether he shared that feeling. His body had seemed to tell her that he did, but there had been no words of confirmation. She tensed, her pliant body pulling away from him.

"What's wrong?" he asked drowsily. "Where're you going?"

"Oh, I don't know," she answered, moving restively to sit on the side of the bed. She cast about desperately for something, anything, to talk about besides the turmoil of love and insecurity inside her. "Are you hungry?"

"Not anymore."

The teasing suggestiveness of his tone and the provocative meaning of the words themselves cut into her, and she flashed a quick glance at him over her shoulder. His casual smile was sexy; his brown eyes were glinting rakishly at her. She saw nothing at all of her own serious feelings reflected in them; he looked totally satisfied and untroubled.

Quickly she turned away to stare at the green and brown wall of the mountain outside. She sat without moving for a long instant, the flippant lightness of his voice echoing in her ears while her thoughts raced.

Her fear was well founded. She loved Vance, but he didn't love her. These last few hours had been the most precious of her entire life, but for him they'd been nothing but a way to assuage the hunger of his body.

The dozens of shades of green in the leaves so close outside the window blurred into a haze as tears began to fill her eyes. The pain grew until it was a physical presence in the pit of her stomach and her limbs felt too heavy to move.

She'd been afraid all along that she was just a distraction for him, and now she had to admit that it was true. He'd held her in his arms, he'd learned every intimate detail of her body, and he knew how to give her more physical pleasure than she'd ever thought possible, but he hadn't the slightest inkling of what was in her heart.

She felt cold in spite of the hot, humid day, and she felt a distance between them, although they were still close enough to touch. She felt abandoned, betrayed; the rich, silent communication of the night before had been destroyed by two words.

She'd thought she couldn't leave him unless she knew they'd be together again, but she could. She had to. She had to get away from this pain.

She reached for the sheet and wrapped it around her, moving swiftly to pick up her dress and underthings.

"I need to go," she announced, trying to keep her voice even. "It's getting late."

"What're you doing?" he protested, sitting up quickly in surprise. "You can't go now. I'm going to make you one of my famous omelets and—"

"Oh, so you cook here, too?" She cut him off harshly, unable to bear his calm tone, his assumption that nothing had happened. Everything between them had been destroyed, and he didn't even know it! Which just went to show that there hadn't been much there in the first place, she told herself furiously.

She avoided looking at him as she moved a chair to search for her sandals. "Do you keep this cottage all the time just for these occasions, or did you rush into the office and rent it when you saw me in the dining room last night?"

"I keep it all the time for business associates and employees who travel to Covey," he answered. His voice was low and evenly controlled, but it had lost its calmness. Now it was touched with anger in response to the sarcasm in hers.

She bent to pick up one shoe, and her eyes followed the circle of burned-out candles on the floor. The wax had dripped down their sides and formed pools beneath them, and their black wicks were tilted at crazy angles in their shapelessness.

Suddenly the ruined candles were a perfect symbol for the way she felt. The entire evening that had been so wonderful, the magical morning that had touched her to the depths, the oneness that she had felt in his arms, were all nothing but travesties. They had no meaning if she were the only one touched by them, and she knew now that none of it meant anything to him. She was probably only one of many girls he had brought to this candlelit room. How many other times had he said, "I just had to see you in the candlelight"?

"Well, it certainly is convenient," she said bitterly, throwing the words at him over her shoulder as she disappeared into the bathroom. "But then, I should have expected good planning from such an efficient businessman."

She dressed quickly, blindly, feeling totally ridiculous putting on the disheveled mauve silk dress again. She took the comb from her little purse and tried to bring some order to her hair, but finally she gave up and ran her hands through it until it was a wild mane around her face and falling to her shoulders. She wanted to put it up, but she had no pins and she wasn't about to go out and scramble around looking for the ones Vance had taken out of it the night before.

She fought down the knot of pain in her stomach as she picked up her purse and stepped quickly out into the room. She was wishing that Vance would be gone; she never wanted to see him again. All she wanted was to escape, escape from that room and from the memories it held.

He was waiting for her, though, tense as a cat waiting for its prey. He was leaning casually against the frame of the door to the living room, dressed in only the tan slacks that went with his suit. His broad chest was a sensual ripple of muscles. He turned at the sound of her footsteps, his dark eyes flashing to her face.

She met his gaze quickly, getting a fleeting impression of a deep scowl under the shock of rumpled black hair, but she looked away as he stepped toward her. She couldn't bear to look at him—even with the agony twisting inside her, the handsomeness of his face tore at her heart.

"Look, Lane," he began, "you can't do this. I won't let you. After what we had last night . . ."

"Evidently we each had something different last night," she snapped back at him. "Now move, and let me out of here."

"I will not. This is totally insane, and I intend to find out what's wrong before you go running away."

Her eyes went to his, quickly, painfully, and she looked at him for just a second before she dropped her gaze to her hands.

"I'm not running away. I just don't want to talk about it." Her voice was low, stubborn, closed to him. "I want to get out of here. I want to go home." Tears pushed against her eyelids and tightened her throat.

He stood very still, running a hand through his hair, and when she looked at him again the frown had deepened. His eyes were like pieces of jet. "Damn it!" he burst out in frustration. "This is just what you did the night of the party. One minute you were in my arms and the next you were running off somewhere for no reason at all. Are we going to go through this same stupid scene over and over again, as if we're in some grade Z movie?"

His impatience and the raw anger in his voice lashed into her. "No, we aren't," she snapped. "This is the last time. We aren't going through this or anything else together ever again."

She tried to step around him, but he blocked her path and moved toward her with a lightning-quick motion, taking both her arms in his big hands. His fingers bit into her bare flesh.

"Look at me," he commanded, his voice deep and rough, vibrating with anger. "Look me in the eye because I'm going to say something that you'd better remember."

The force of the feeling emanating from him was almost frightening in its intensity; suddenly he was dangerous, alien. Resentment at the uncompromising order rose in her, mixing with her anger, and she tilted her chin to stare past him, refusing to look into his face.

They stood there, very still, at a standoff for a seemingly endless time. Her heart was beating so painfully that she thought it would burst against her ribs, and the pressure of his iron fingers around her arms was bruising in its fierceness. She was so angry that she didn't think she could contain it, but she wouldn't give him the satisfaction of making her struggle against his superior strength.

Finally his big hand cupped her chin. His touch wasn't rough, but it was incredibly strong, and he tilted her head up inexorably to force her eyes to meet his.

"If you're determined not to talk to me, then go. But remember this: We'll go through at least *one* more thing together because one of these days you're going to give me an explanation!"

He let her go with a suddenness that made her sway a little, dropping his hands abruptly to his sides.

She brushed past him and left the bedroom, almost running across the width of the broad sitting room and out into the stifling heat of the day.

Chapter Twelve

*L*ane paused at the top of the ridge behind Alice's house and sank down onto a large, flat rock at the foot of a giant birch. She had been climbing through the hills for hours until her muscles screamed with pain, and she was using that hurt to dull the one in her heart.

She leaned back against the tree's broad trunk and caught her breath, staring down toward Covey. She could see glimpses of the old house and a few of the town's other buildings through the thick leaves. She needed to get back, she thought. Soon dusk would be coming on, and it would be hard for her to find her way over the rocky terrain.

But she wasn't ready to be with anyone yet, not even the quietly understanding Alice. She had been so relieved to find no one home when she'd returned at noon, and she still felt that she had to have solitude. She needed at least a year without any distractions, she thought wryly, to try to sort out the chaos that Vance had created inside her.

She had tried not to think about it while she stood in the warm shower and scrubbed his touch from her skin. She'd forced it out of her mind while she wove her wet hair into one long braid and pulled on her faded jeans and cotton tee shirt, then tied on a bandanna for a headband. She'd blotted it out while she'd tramped all over both sides of the ridge, trying to interest herself in the summer foliage of the beeches and laurels, the rocks covered with lichen, the wild blue phlox and the deep green of the rhododendron along the mossy brooks.

But now that she was exhausted, now that she hardly had the physical strength left to get back to the house, she had no energy to hold the agony back, and it all came flooding over her again. She stared blindly down through the maze of green and absently touched her lips, still bruised from Vance's kisses.

The memory of his mouth touching hers and the weight of his long body on hers brought back all the sensations of the night with him, and her mind began to whirl as it vividly replayed one sensual scene after another. She had never felt so happy, so secure, so safe, in her life as she had felt in his arms. And she had never known that such rapture could exist.

She straightened suddenly, the rough bark of the tree trunk scraping her skin through the thin shirt. How could she lose herself in these blissful imaginings when he had hurt her so? Vance didn't love her, and if she wanted to survive, she'd better not let herself love him, either.

Impatiently she got up and started headlong down the steep side of the ridge. She didn't want to be alone after all, not with those memories to haunt her.

Even though she moved carelessly, quickly, through the forest, without letting anything really slow her down, by the time she reached the bottom of the hill it was beginning to get dark. She walked rapidly along the edge of the rocky creek and then crossed it, her hiking boots echoing hollowly on the wooden bridge.

The sound was a lonely one, and she could see no one else around. Suddenly she felt terribly bereft, alone in a way that she had never been until she'd felt so close to Vance. Her lips twisted bitterly at the thought. That closeness had been nothing but an illusion.

She was approaching the house from the back, and since the lights were on in the kitchen she went in through the back door. She had to talk to someone—she had to find Alice.

"Hi, Alice."

Alice turned from the stove, where she was stirring a skillet full of frying potatoes, her smile a warm welcome. "Hi, Lane." She gestured with her spatula. "Well, now, you've come in the back way and missed your visitor."

The words were so unexpected that it took a minute for them to register. "What visitor? Who is it?"

Alice's eyes twinkled merrily. "Reckon it must be that brown-eyed, handsome man we was talking about yesterday."

Lane stared at her. Vance! Vance was there!

"He's setting out in the front porch swing,

waiting for you to come home. Said he'd ruther be outside than to wait in the living room."

Lane's heart thudded against her ribs. She *couldn't* see him now and give him the explanation he'd demanded that morning!

She rested her hand on one of the ladder-back chairs, her mind whirling. There would never be a time to explain her behavior to him, she realized. How could she possibly say, "I left so quickly because I love you and I realized that you don't love me"?

"Oh, Alice," she said finally, trying to sound casual. "Do you think you could tell him that . . . that I've called to say that I'm not coming home tonight?"

"Nope." Alice shook her head decisively and turned back to her potatoes. "He said he's staying 'til he sees you, and he is. I know a bound-and-determined man when I see one."

"But . . ."

"Go get it over with, hon. Whatever's wrong between you two, go get it out and settle it. Then you all come on in here and eat supper with me. Rowena's gone up to Charlie's with Thad."

Lane thought about the moment when she'd left Vance that morning. The obstinate determination in his voice as he'd told her that he was going to get an explanation echoed in her ears. She sighed. Alice was right. If he'd said he was staying until he saw her, he was staying.

She walked through the house slowly, reluctantly, and when she reached the front door she stood for a minute just inside it, hoping against hope that he had gone. The slow creak of the swing floated to her, though, and she sighed and pushed the screen open.

She'd see him; she had no choice. She'd tell him to go, and he could forget about his explanation. And she could forget about him.

He stood as she walked out into the darkness of the porch. "Hi, Lane."

The rich tones of his voice affected her nerve endings as if his hand had moved over her skin. She straightened her back and stood very still.

He indicated the place beside him. "Come sit by me."

"No, thanks. I'll stand."

He stiffened. "I was hoping you'd be more rational by now."

"I am. It was last night when I was out of my mind."

Slowly, deliberately, he walked over to lean against one of the posts, positioning himself so that he could see her face in the faint light that spilled out through the doorway. It fell on to him, too, throwing the planes of his face into shadow. Her eyes locked with his.

"Lane, you've put me through hell today." The flat statement fell into the quiet night. "If I've done something to upset you, I have a right to know what it is."

She stared back at him, into the dark pools of his eyes, into the mysterious depths that pulled her to him as if they had magnetic powers. She wanted to say something, anything, that would break that spell and make him leave her alone, but her mind refused to function.

He waited for her to speak, and when she didn't

he held out his hand. "Lane, I want you. You know that."

She couldn't look away from him; she couldn't move away. The very fact of his just being near her, the inescapable sexual attraction that had always been between them, held her as if she were physically bound to him. The warm, masculine scent of him was filling her senses, and she was aching with the memory of their lovemaking.

So she put her hand into his and went to him as if she had no other choice. Suddenly, unaccountably, in spite of the hours of anguish she had just been through, she wanted him, too.

He smiled down at her. Then he let go of her hand and with both of his he cupped her small waist, pulling her just close enough to him so that the tips of her breasts barely touched his chest.

Without a word he bent to kiss her upturned face, his lips meeting hers with a gentleness that stripped away all her defenses. They tasted hers, questioned hers, and lured hers until she moved one step closer to him and put her arms around his neck.

He pressed her against him passionately, crushing his mouth onto hers in a deep, thrusting kiss. He forced her lips apart and held her in an embrace that seared her entire body.

Desperately she twisted her mouth away from his. "No," she whispered. "No, I can't. . . ."

His lips found hers again and silenced her with unerring swiftness. One hand slid up over her back to press her against him, and he cradled her head with the other.

She felt the crispness of his hair between her fingers as she instinctively pulled his head even closer, and her hand traced across the breadth of his shoulders and down the hollow of his back, as if her fears had no foundation. They didn't exist anymore; nothing existed except her love for him.

Her lips opened for him, and his tongue took possession of her mouth again, teasing and tantalizing her, reaching into the depths of her, until her already bruised lips clung desperately to his. Then his hand moved up her narrow rib cage to cup her breast, and the flames of desire began to leap and burn in every vein in her body.

The terror came back with it. She tore her mouth away from his and pulled back, but he kept her within the circle of his arms.

"Vance," she began breathlessly, "we have to stop this. We can't see each other again. . . ."

He stared at her incredulously for a moment, almost visibly assimilating the words. "Then, whatever this is, it's really serious," he said, his voice strangely flat.

She nodded, her ability to speak suddenly gone again.

His hands moved to her shoulders and, holding them very gently, he said, "Let's go somewhere and talk this all out. Let's go for a ride."

She didn't answer. Desire for him and fear for herself were warring inside her; despair that he didn't love her was tearing her apart. He had said "Lane, I want you," not "Lane, I love you." She raised her hand to adjust her headband and realized that she was trembling.

He spoke again, soothingly, gently, as if she were a fractious horse that might bolt at any minute. "I'm on my way up to Old Man Charlie's," he said. "You can ride up there with me, and we'll talk out this mysterious problem on the way." He turned, keeping one arm around her shoulders, and began walking her toward the steps, just as if she had agreed to go.

She hardly noticed; her mind grasped at the new topic of conversation. It was better to talk about anything rather than these wild, terrible feelings.

She took a ragged breath and managed to speak. "Why are you going to Charlie's?"

"I'm going to make him an offer for permission to use the story he told us."

She stopped stock-still at the top of the steps. "You can't do that!" She pulled away from him and looked up into his eyes in disbelief. "Vance, I've explained that to you before. Please don't. You'll insult Charlie."

He shook his head. "I don't think so. He can use the money, and we can sure use the story. Those pictures—the waterfall and Charlie's barn and cabin—will attract more attention than just about anything else we're planning."

Abhorrence washed over her in a cold wave. This proved it beyond all doubt. There was no way he could love her. He was getting ready to make their special place, their waterfall, public property. And he would alienate Charlie, who had trusted them both.

Hot anger began to rise in her, and all the words she hadn't been able to find for him rushed to her tongue. "If you go through with this you'll be slapping Charlie in the face, and you'll ruin yourself, and me, too, all over these mountains! Everyone will say that Rowena was right and that we are working together!"

She tried to force herself to sound calm as she said imploringly, "Vance, Charlie told us that story in confidence, in the spirit of friendship, and he said plainly that he didn't want us to tell it to anyone else."

"But I don't think he knows how much money is involved. If he knew that and really thought about what it could do . . ."

"Money!" She almost screamed the word. "I'm not talking about money. I'm trying to talk to you about the betrayal of a confidence and friendship from a man who doesn't offer these things lightly!"

"Lane, you don't understand. . . ."

The heat of her anger gave way to cold fury as he moved to the step just below her. Their eyes were almost on a level. She stared into his with a strength she didn't know she possessed.

"Yes I do." She bit off each word with terrible precision. "I understand that you have no compunction about exploiting people less sophisticated than you. I also understand that you are interested in me for whatever help I can give you in that exploitation and"—she almost faltered—"and because of the physical attraction between us."

She paused to take a deep, steadying breath, then went on. "But there's something *you* need to understand. I'm not interested in participating in your little schemes. And, since their very existence points up the infinite amount of distance that there is between us, I think we should consider this our last meeting. I won't see you again."

He stared back at her, his face an impenetrable mask, drawn with anger. He didn't move at all; it was almost as if he had suddenly turned himself to stone, but his eyes were alive. They were alive and full of a riot of feelings; they were searching hers for the reasons behind her words.

The sincerity of the quest that she saw there, the force of the hurt that he couldn't keep from showing, drew the truth from her.

"I have to have something that will last, Vance," she told him slowly, her voice low and full of pain. "Something that I can depend on. A passion like ours is too much for me to handle if it's just a temporary amusement for you. It has to be a permanent part of my life, and it has to be based on real love, or I don't want it at all."

Before he could answer she turned away and went into the house, letting the screen door close behind her.

Lane put the last of the seven whimsically carved wooden hillsmen on the glass top of the counter and turned to Alice. "What else can I do to help?"

"Not another thing. Just set down over there and visit with me." Alice propped open the front door of the little shop as she spoke. "Law, it's hot in here."

"Alice, let me help you with something else. I can't just sit around. I have to *do* something."

Alice fixed her with an appraising stare as she walked back to the counter filled with toys.

"No, you rest. You've been running around like a chicken with its head cut off for the last three days, doing all your work and half of mine. You've got to ease up. Everything'll be all right; you'll see."

Alice watched maternally until Lane sank onto

the oak stool behind the counter and pretended to relax; then she went back to arranging the small wooden toys inside the glass counter. Her eyes were on them, but she kept up a steady stream of words directed at Lane.

"Now you just remember this—if he's the one meant for you, he'll come back and you'll work out your problems. And if he's not, it's a whole lot better to find it out now than after you're married and it's too late."

Lane stared at her incredulously for a moment, then chuckled wryly. "Alice, you are so funny. There's never been any mention of marriage between Vance and me."

Alice flashed a keen glance at her.

"Well, there hasn't," Lane said defensively.

"No, and there's a whole more that hasn't been mentioned, either. But I've lived a long time, and I know a lovers' quarrel when I see one."

Lane shook her head, and her lips twisted in an ironic smile. "Not exactly. I haven't heard a word from him in days, and I don't expect to. I'll never even see him again, so you can't exactly call that a lovers' quarrel."

Her voice was even and steady, but the words made her tremble inside. Alice was right. She had been rushing around like a madwoman since the last time she'd seen Vance, trying to keep so busy that she couldn't think about him. She'd realized how much she loved him and then lost him forever, all in the space of a few hours, and she felt as if she'd been through an emotional shredder.

The hurt that was beginning to be a familiar part of her life twisted in her again. It had been three days, and Vance hadn't even tried to call. What she had said to Alice was true—they wouldn't be seeing each other again. And that was for the best.

She felt her face grow warm as those last few minutes with him flashed into her memory. She only wished that she hadn't told him the truth about how deep her feelings ran for him. If she hadn't, at least she'd have her pride.

"What we need to do right now is to get your mind on something else," Alice went on as if Lane hadn't spoken. "Rowena wants Thad to come to supper tomorrow night."

"But, Alice, are you ready for that?"

"I reckon so." Alice sighed deeply. "I'd just as well get ready for it, 'cause he's gonna be part of the family."

"He is? Is it official? When did all this happen?" Lane felt her face break into a genuine smile for the first time in days. "I can't believe this!"

"It's not exactly official yet. They're planning to make the big announcement at the Appalachia Day Celebration two weeks from Saturday, so don't tell anybody yet."

"OK, I won't."

"They came to me last night while you was gone to that singing in Whitesburg," Alice continued thoughtfully, as if she were trying to explain it all to herself as well as to Lane. "We all talked for a long time, and I gave them my blessing." She sighed and stared out unseeingly at the street. "I couldn't do nothing else, and I'm hoping it'll all work out."

"I really think it will, Alice. I imagine that Thad's ready to settle down, and Rowena's always been crazy about him."

Alice nodded. "And he is a likeable boy. You were right about that."

"Right about what?" a cheerful female voice chimed in from the open doorway, and they turned to see Rowena, standing in the circle of Thad's arm.

"And who's a likeable boy?" Thad asked mischievously.

Alice chuckled, the sound a mixture of amusement and chagrin. "Oh, go on with you," she said, making a gesture of dismissal. "How long have you all been standing there, anyhow?"

"Long enough to know all your secrets," he replied. "And now to keep us from tellin' them all over town, you'll have to bribe us with a couple of cold soda pops."

Welcoming the chance to get away for a minute, Lane pushed aside the little curtain and stepped into the back room to get the drinks. Rowena and That had had such hard feelings about her and had hurt her so deeply that any meeting with them was bound to be awkward. They didn't seem resentful now, though. She smiled ironically to herself. Being in love seemed to have mellowed them toward the whole world.

She opened four of the icy cold bottles and took them back out into the shop, handing them around in the sudden silence that fell with her return. She sipped at her drink, and Thad took a swallow of his, then he cleared his throat uncomfortably.

"Lane, Rowena and I, we've got somethin' to say to you," he began.

She glanced at Rowena, who gave her a quick, rather shy smile.

"We want to tell you we're sorry," he went on, the words seeming to come more easily as he proceeded. "We misjudged you and did you some wrong."

Surprised by his directness, Lane stared at him for a moment, then nodded. "Yes, you did."

"It was all my fault." Rowena spoke up in a tone much meeker than was usual for her. "I should've given you a chance to explain instead of running out and bad-mouthing you to the whole county."

Lane met the girl's abashed gaze. "I really wish you had listened to me," she said quietly. "I could have explained everything."

"We know that now," Thad put in. "And I don't think that either one of us will ever be so quick to jump to conclusions again."

Mystified by this complete change in attitude, Lane looked from Thad to Rowena and back again. "This makes me really happy." She stopped and shot a questioning glance at Alice. "But I don't understand. What made you change your minds about me?"

"Alice explained everything to us last night," Thad answered. "When we told her that we wanted to get married she didn't oppose us. We'd expected her to say she'd never agree to it, but she said that you'd helped her see a lot of things, that you'd been for us all the time."

"I also told them that they ought to be ashamed of themselves for not trusting you more," Alice said tartly. "The very idea of listening in on people's private conversations and then running off half-cocked to spread rumors and gossip!"

Rowena blushed painfully. "Aunt Alice told us

what you'd said about your talk with Mr. Morgan that day," she said, forcing herself to meet Lane's eyes. "And now I see that I misunderstood what you all were saying." Her voice trembled, and she dropped her eyes again as soon as she had finished speaking.

Suddenly she seemed painfully young to Lane. Her heart went out to the girl who had been so fiercely loyal to her people. "Well, you've heard stories about the past and you've seen outsiders come in and take advantage of the people around here in your own lifetime. You had some reasons for being suspicious, but you just decided too quickly that I was one of 'them.'"

Rowena nodded her agreement, but she was too choked up to speak.

"Lane, will you forgive us?" Thad asked. "I feel really bad about all this."

A sudden happiness that everything was finally all right between them at last filled her. "I'll think about it," she teased. "You two might invite me to your engagement party, and I could give you my answer then."

He chuckled happily, the old twinkle back in his eyes. "We'll do it. It's going to be quite a shindig—we're going to make the announcement at the Appalachia Day Celebration and then dance all night!" He grinned at her, and the old camaraderie was in the air again. "Promise me right now you'll dance with me, OK?"

She promised, and Rowena chimed in with, "Maybe if everyone sees us together on Appalachia Day we can undo some of the damage we did to you, Lane. At least, we can try."

She agreed to that, and they made plans to meet at the bandstand at noon so that she would be present for their big announcement. They all chatted for a few minutes more, then Thad and Rowena left, walking hand in hand down the street toward his shop.

After they'd gone several customers came in to keep Alice busy and, since she wanted to be alone, Lane hastily waved good-bye. She went out into the heat of the afternoon, hardly aware of the discomfort, just needing a long walk so she could sort things out.

It felt good to be friends with Thad and Rowena again, but she was wishing that she hadn't promised to go to the Appalachia Day Celebration. It would be an exciting day, a truly festive occasion, and there was no way she would be in the mood for that.

She walked slowly along the main street, climbing up and down the hilly sidewalks without really noticing where she was going. She had forgotten about Appalachia Day during the last few days, as a matter of fact, but there had been a time not too long ago when she'd thought how great it would be to attend with Vance.

The celebration was the big event of the year, always held on the picturesque campus of the tiny junior college in Whitesburg. People from all over that part of the southern mountains met there to show off and share their music and crafts; it was like an enormous county fair established for the purpose of celebrating their mutual heritage.

It usually attracted several hundred "outsiders," too, who came early and stayed until long after dark listening to music and dancing, sampling the

wares of the food booths and buying the handcraft-
ed items that were for sale.

It would have been a perfect time to introduce
Vance to a wide variety of things inherent in
mountain life and a perfectly romantic place to be
with him. Thad and Rowena would be together,
there'd be other couples wandering through the
grounds with their arms around each other, and she
would miss Vance even more than she was doing
now.

Without consciously thinking about where she
was or what her destination would be, she finally
found herself walking alongside the noisy creek to
Alice's house. She went slowly up the walk and
dropped down on the porch steps, reluctant to
enter the lonely rooms.

A breeze had sprung up, a cool wispyness in the
air that was a refreshing change from the close heat
that had clung to the hills all day, and she tilted her
head back against the post and lifted her cheeks to
it.

The afternoon sun was beginning to fade, but
there was still plenty of light, and she watched the
shades of blue and gray in the clouds against the
ever-changing face of Big Caney. It reminded her
of the afternoon when she'd sat in that very spot
and listened as Alice told her the story of her love
for Jason Campbell.

Lane's lips trembled and tears sprang to her eyes
as she thought of the instinctive fear she'd had that
day—the fear that Vance would break her heart.
And so he had.

She brushed at the tears and shook her head,
smiling to herself with bitter irony. Alice had been
so worried about Thad and Rowena, and they were

probably going to be the happiest couple in Covey. It was she and Vance who were just as star-crossed as Jason and Alice had been.

She would end up just like Alice—she would still be in love with Vance Morgan when she was sixty, and that love would be just as hopeless as Alice's love for Jason had always been.

Chapter Thirteen

Lane pulled the jeep into a narrow space between two cars parked across the road from the college and turned off the ignition. She dropped her keys into her roomy straw bag and got out, smoothing her full dirndl skirt as she stood waiting for some cars to pass. It was almost ten o'clock, and the celebration had officially begun at eight, but people were still streaming onto the campus.

She crossed the road quickly, her flat leather sandals tapping lightly on its hard surface. She stopped for a minute on the bridge that spanned the ever-present creek while a young couple with two excited children crowded past her.

She looked around, wondering where to go first, what to do during the time before she was to meet Thad and Rowena. In spite of the sincerity of their invitation and their desire to make things up to her, she didn't want to spend all morning with them.

She was still dreading this day, although in the ten days or so since she'd agreed to come she had decided that she wouldn't think of it as a social occasion. She would just consider it a part of her job and try to make some new contacts for the two months left of her grant.

Thank goodness she had finally been able to concentrate more on her work lately. The burning memories of Vance were still tearing her apart, but she had learned to work in spite of them. She had to, she thought, because they were something she would be living with for the rest of her life.

She ran her eyes over the campus again, forcing herself to think about what she saw. She'd always liked it; it was one of the prettiest places in East Kentucky, with its mixture of old and new stone buildings scattered up and down the creek on all levels of the hillside. And today it was even more picturesque than usual, with colorful booths set up among the trees in every spot where the ground was flat enough.

Finally she chose the winding path to the right, the one that went by the tiny one-room cabin that had been the first school building in the Booker Creek Valley. She followed it, walking between the scattered birches and elms with a talkative group of visitors carrying cameras and tape recorders.

There was a large flat area on the other side of the trees and beyond the science building, and she knew that the bandstand and wooden dance floor would be set up there. Still more booths would be surrounding them, especially the ones that needed more space, like those for the yarn-dyeing and blacksmithing demonstrations, and she could start by exploring them.

But when she came out of the trees and down the hillside onto the grassy lawn, all her plans for efficiency melted away. She wandered in and out among the booths and the people without any purpose at all.

She saw several people that she knew, and they smiled at her and called to her warmly; evidently they were beginning to see that Rowena had been wrong in her accusations. They were making her feel very welcome, and that was a comfort, but the hollow loneliness that had been filling her for days wouldn't go away.

Addie Keanan was dyeing yarn, stirring it in a pot over a small fire and hanging the vivid orange strands on a line that she'd strung from her booth to a tree. Lane considered going over to talk with her about it. She knew that she really should ask the woman some questions and make some notes about the process she was using, but somehow she just couldn't find the motivation.

She drifted over to speak to Andy Johnson as he deftly bound switches of broomcorn into brooms and tied them with red and green twine; then she stopped at Sarah Ashe's pottery stall, running her fingers over the smooth surfaces of the vases and bowls as they chatted.

"Lane!"

She turned to see Polly Clay, ensconced behind a quilting frame, beckoning to her with a gnarled hand. Lane walked toward Polly's booth, forcing a smile to her lips.

"How are you, Polly?" she asked. "I've been intending to come see you again."

The old woman nodded. "You do that, now." She looked Lane over carefully from head to toe, her hand hovering in the air over the navy blue and gold fabric of her work, her thimble glinting in the sunlight. "You're gettin' too thin, child. What's the matter? That Glory woman been a'follerin' you around all this time?"

Lane chuckled dryly, but her heart twisted. Vance was probably with Gloria that very minute.

"No," she answered. "I guess I've just been working hard."

Polly smiled. "Well, you look mighty pretty anyhow. Them is yore colors."

Lane glanced down at the outfit she had put on that morning practically without thinking. It was very simple: a low-necked, ruffled blouse of rich, buttercup yellow that matched her shining hair and a polished cotton skirt in a blue and yellow print. She supposed she had lost weight—the narrow wraparound belt had gone around her waist twice and there were still long streamers left.

It was no wonder; she hadn't wanted to eat for a long time. She hadn't wanted to eat or sleep; she hadn't wanted to work. In fact, it seemed that for all her life she had wanted nothing but Vance. And she had driven him away. She had told him that she wouldn't see him again, and he had taken her at her word. It had been almost three weeks, and he hadn't even tried to contact her.

But it was for the best. Her thoughts began going around and around in their well-worn pattern. What good would it have done to continue those heavenly nights in his arms when it would have all ended when she went back to the university? Alice had been right. Better now than later.

"Matter of fact, I reckon I'll have to give this

here quilt to you," Polly went on. "Its colors is kin to them."

"That'd be great," Lane agreed, putting her mind on what she was saying with an effort. "I'd love it. And I'd also love to do that taped interview we tried for. When are you going to give it to me?"

"Any time," Polly replied cheerfully, as if she'd never been difficult about it at all. "Just come on up to the house when you get a chance."

Lane accepted this calmly, as if she'd expected just that answer, and after chatting with Polly for a few more minutes she wandered away again. She felt a brief moment of elation that she'd get her tape after all, but the memories of Vance that had been pulling at her were coming back in full force and suddenly they seemed to soak up all her ability to care.

Suddenly she was acutely sensitive, her nerves raw, her senses unable to cope. The vivid orange shades of Addie's yarn seemed too bright, and so did the sunlight on the open meadow. The strains of fiddle music from the band already gathered on the bandstand were too cheerful, and the merry voices of the crowd were too loud. How could everyone be so happy? How could the morning air be so crisp and the atmosphere so festive? Didn't they know that Vance was gone from her and he'd never come back?

She had to get away from the festive atmosphere; she had to be alone for a while. She climbed back up the hill, but just at the edge of the tree-lined path a voice called to her. Old Man Charlie Campbell was sitting on a bench that had been built around the trunk of a big pine tree.

"How are ye, girl?" he asked, leaning his head back so that he could squint up at her from underneath the brim of his hat. "Ain't seen ye fer a while."

He patted the seat beside him, and she sat down. She felt as if she were going to burst into tears, as if she couldn't possibly deal with him at that particular moment.

What was he going to say? How did he feel toward her since Vance's offer to buy his story? Was he going to tell her that Rowena had been right, that she was a fake and a money-grubber working for Vance, that both of them had betrayed him by wanting to make public the story he'd told them in confidence?

She couldn't stand it if he did. She really loved the old man; she admired him, and she wanted his respect.

They sat quietly for a long moment, looking down at the festivities below, listening to the mournful bluegrass music from a band that she recognized as Thad's.

"Pretty good music-makers, ain't they?" he said at last.

"Yes, they are."

"That Thad. Seems like jist a day or so ago he was about this high." He held out a worn, steady hand about three feet from the ground. "And now he's a'gonna go and git married."

"I know. And I'm really happy for them." Lane looked down, playing absently with the string handle of her purse.

Old Man shifted the tobacco in his jaw and stared down at the crowd. Then he spoke in his slow, calm way. "And do you reckon there might even be another weddin' around here one of these days?"

The confident, congratulatory tone in his voice seemed to carry some hidden message, and she looked up, startled, into his twinkling blue gaze. "Charlie, what are you talking about?"

He inclined his head in the direction of the convivial scene below. "Yonder comes yore young man now."

Her heart heard the words and understood their meaning long before her mind did. Her pulse stopped completely for a long second, then began to beat again, slowly, painfully, an unreasoning thrill coursing through her veins.

Then she remembered her own words: "I won't see you again." Vance might be there, but he wasn't there to see her.

Her heart breaking, she turned her head slowly and looked down into the meadow. He was coming toward them, moving with his long, clean stride across the grass and up the hillside. Her eyes clung to him as he moved in and out among the trees, the beams of sunlight that filtered through them glinting off his thick dark hair and pointing up the classic angles of his face. She couldn't bear it if she couldn't touch him again!

Then he reached them, and the warmth in his brown eyes touched both her and Charlie.

"Are these the best seats in the house?" His voice was deep, as rich as she had remembered it, and the familiar thrill went down her spine. "Maybe I ought to join you—looks like quite a show shaping up."

Charlie harrumphed his agreement, but Lane looked up at Vance without speaking. Her resolve not to see him again revolved in her mind, but her body was yearning uncontrollably for his, and when he propped his hand against the big trunk of the tree and put one knee on the bench his leg brushed hers and she was on fire.

His eyes bored into hers. "Lane," he said casually, "how've you been?"

At last she managed one word. "Fine."

His eyes held hers, their look deep and dark, unfathomable, yet glowing with something new, something strong and exciting that she couldn't identify. They were giving her a message that she couldn't read.

And a caress. Her breath shortened, and her lips parted involuntarily. It was almost as if she could feel his kiss.

Then the touch of his eyes was gone; he was looking at Charlie, and she felt as if she were a child deserted in a strange place.

"Charlie, you were right," Vance was saying, a comfortable, teasing note in his voice. "You didn't want to come to New York with me after all. It was just as full of traffic and people as you said it'd be."

Her heart stopped for a second. He'd been gone! He'd been in New York! That was why she hadn't heard from him.

But there were telephones in New York. He could have called her. She hadn't heard from him because she'd told him not to call.

Dazed by her thoughts and the opposing emotions rioting inside her, Lane only half listened to the conversation. Enough of it registered, though, for her to realize that Charlie wasn't angry with Vance. He didn't act as if Vance had insulted him the last time they had met.

Then Vance's elbow was resting on his knee, his hand was on her shoulder, and she felt as if she would never move again. "Lane, let's go for a walk. We need to talk."

She didn't want to talk. She'd already told him far too much about her feelings for him, and he had told her nothing in return.

But she wanted to be alone with him. Her body was crying for some privacy so that she could touch him and feel his lips on hers just one more time. Then they could say good-bye again, this time forever.

She stood and looked down at Charlie. "I'll see you. . . ."

"Lane, Grandpa Charlie, come on. It's almost time! We're going to make the announcement when Thad finishes this song."

Rowena was beckoning to them from halfway up the gently sloping hillside, seemingly torn between coming to get them and getting too far away from her beloved Thad.

Disappointment twisted in Lane; she needed to be with Vance. She couldn't think about anything else. But this announcement was the reason why she'd come, and she couldn't disappoint Thad and Rowena. Not now, especially, when they were getting to be friends again.

Vance was looking at her, a question in his eyes. "Thad and Rowena are going to announce their engagement," she explained. "I promised to be here for that."

"Who ever heered of makin' sich a big deal out of gittin' married?" Charlie grumbled, but he sounded fairly cheerful about it, and he got up and started down toward the wooden stage.

Vance and Lane followed, and when her sandals slipped on the grassy slope he put his arm around her waist. He kept it there even after they'd reached the bottom and had joined Alice and Thad's other relatives, and she couldn't keep from settling into the curve of his arm, her entire being thrilling with the excitement of his nearness.

Thad pulled Rowena up onto the stage with him, and with his band softly playing a love song in the background, he told the world that they were in love and planned to be married. Lane smiled up into their glowing faces, and then at Vance, her eyes full of happiness for them.

She looked around at all the friends and relatives who were gathered to support them in their intention to spend the rest of their lives together, and saw the same expression on their faces. This was something that was as old as the mountains that enclosed them, and she had a feeling that their love was going to last as long as they lived.

Tears sprang to her eyes as Vance's arm tightened around her. Oh, why couldn't it be that way for them, too? It was such a shame to waste the fiery magic that flared between them. But if she couldn't have at least the hope of permanence, she didn't want this ecstasy at all.

They joined the group around Thad and Rowena, the men shaking Thad's hand and slapping him on the back and kissing Rowena, the women hugging them both and wishing them happiness. Then, in just a few minutes, the fiddles began to cry out, loud and fast, and the dance floor magically cleared except for a square of dancers whose feet began a cheerful beat on the wooden boards.

"Now, enough of this togetherness," Vance whispered in her ear. "I want you all to myself."

He pulled her even closer to his side and began to work their way through the crowd. Soon they were free and climbing out of the little valley to reach a path that ran higher up along the hillside back to the main part of the campus. In places the path was so narrow that they walked single file, Vance going ahead and reaching back to steady her on the crude rocks that formed steps between the levels, so they hardly talked at all.

With the last group of steps they came to the rambling old dining hall. A wide porch surrounded it on three sides, filled with ancient caned chairs and loveseats. Not a soul was around; evidently the celebrants who hadn't remained near the center of the festivities were too lazy to climb so far.

"This looks like a comfortable place to talk," Vance remarked as he reached for her hand and led her up the creaking steps and over to one of the loveseats.

She sat down, her body sinking into the curve worn by hundreds of others who'd sat there before, and he sat beside her, casually laying one arm along the back. Suddenly, now that they were out of the crowd, it wasn't so easy to have him touch her. It was as if a touch might lead to something more, and she wasn't ready for that.

He looked into her face, and suddenly, desperately, she wanted to postpone whatever he was going to say. She didn't want them to talk and decide that it really *was* better not to see each other anymore. She just wanted to be with him for a little while longer, to sit on the shady old porch and look at him, to take in the shape of his face and the angle of his cheekbones in the dappled light that fell through the trees.

His long legs, encased in tight, faded jeans, were crossed toward her, his knees touching hers lightly in the small space. She followed their lean lines up to the tooled leather belt that circled his slim waist and the pale yellow oxford cloth shirt that made his eyes seem like dark brown velvet. The tiny creases that feathered out from them seemed deeper than they'd been the last time she'd seen him, and his soft, thick hair was a little longer, a little more casual.

Hungrily she drank in the sight of him, the warm nearness of him. Everything about him was something to remember—everything about him was something to touch. Instinctively her hands moved to caress him; they ached to actually feel his skin, his hair.

Yet she didn't dare let herself. She gripped the woven arm of the old seat, unconsciously running the tips of her fingers over its roughness.

Finally she tore her eyes from the lock of black hair that had fallen across his forehead and forced her gaze on to the shimmering green of the mountainside. Still she could see nothing but the sensual shape of his face.

Desperately she tried to think of something to say.

He didn't say a word and he didn't touch her, but she turned back so her eyes could find his again, drawn by the physical attraction that vibrated between them, the inexplicable magnetism that had been there since the moment they met.

His gaze was warmer than the sunlight against their faces, and in spite of all the doubts that were plaguing her, it pulled at the core of her. Heat spread through her veins.

His hand moved from the back of the seat to her shoulder and slid down her bare arm in a wordless caress. She felt her lips tremble with desire as he held her eyes locked with his. Then he bent toward her.

He kissed her gently at first, tasting each tiny section of her mouth separately, tenderly—first the middle of her lips, then each corner, then the outline of the lower one. She sat very still, transfixed by the delicate touch, so amazed by the loving that was springing back to life inside her that she couldn't move.

He drew back and looked at her, his eyes questioning, searching hers.

Again his lips came back to the midpoint of her mouth, this time hungrily, and his tongue traced the edge of the opening, asking to be let in. That request flowed through her lips to all the muscles in her body, and at last she could move again.

She parted her lips for him and at the same time she slipped her arms around his neck; she couldn't bear to be apart from him any longer. She loved him, she wanted him, and if this were going to be the last time she saw him, she was going to let him know that.

Her tongue met his and touched it quickly, then moved away. His followed hers, touching and stroking, and hers came back eagerly to meet it. He explored her mouth, took it for his own, caressed it as if he were famished, and she melted into him the way she had the first time he had kissed her.

All thought left her, all her fears, and instinctively she put her hand behind his head and pulled him even closer, as if she were afraid that this wonder was going to stop. She was filled with joy at being with him again, and as the softness of her breasts pressed against his hard chest she thought she could never get enough.

The hard breadth of his hand was warm against her back, holding her nearer; suddenly he pulled away to put the tiniest space between them. Then his hand was at her waist, sliding up her rib cage to cup the high fullness of her breast.

At first she leaned into him, wanting him, but as his thumb brushed the swollen tip of her breast beneath the thin cotton of her blouse, pure fear knifed through her. Her skin was clamoring for the sensation of being next to his, she wanted his hands on her, but he had brought her there to say good-bye. This was the last time she would see him, and she couldn't bear it.

She made a little cry deep in her throat and tried to pull away from him. She moved back slightly, and his hand left her breast.

It didn't follow her, but his lips did; they didn't permit any space to appear between his mouth and hers. They still drank her in thirstily; they pleaded with her and tantalized her; they wouldn't let her go. She was afraid of the feelings pulsing through her, but didn't have the strength to push away from him completely.

He held the kiss and gently stroked her back and arm until she relaxed in his warmth, in his closeness. When at last they pulled apart she took a deep, ragged breath, and he pulled her head to his chest, cradling it there with one big hand. She lay against him, trying to just be with him and to savor his nearness without letting herself think about him. She took pleasure in the breadth of his muscular chest and listened to the rapid beating of his heart.

"Lane . . ."

No. She couldn't let him talk now. She didn't want to hear that this was the last time they'd be like this. Not yet.

She put one finger across his lips and tried desperately to think of something to distract him. Finally she said, "Well, I seem to have been wrong about one thing."

His eyes glinted at her mischievously, full of a secret. "You probably were wrong about more than one, but go ahead and tell me."

"Charlie. He certainly didn't act as if you'd insulted him. In fact, you two seem to be the best of buddies."

"We are. We understand each other."

"So you *did* go up there that night and make him the offer." She cringed inside at the words "that night," and a shadow of the suffering she'd gone through since then fell across them.

He tightened his arms around her as if he sensed it. "I did. And that visit changed my life."

Her eyes widened and flew to his, searching,

questioning, full of the loneliness she'd felt without him.

He began to speak slowly, thoughtfully, rocking her slightly in his arms. "I really shouldn't give Charlie *all* the credit, though. I should've said that *you* and Charlie have changed my life."

She raised her head again in surprise, and his arms tightened around her, as if he were afraid that she would move even more. His arms held the same message his lips had: He was claiming her. But how could that be?

"Vance, what are you talking about?"

"When I left you that night I was furious. Furious and confused and determined to make a deal with Charlie no matter what you said. I thought that the appeal of money would be the same everywhere—I just knew that you were wrong."

He moved just a little to settle her into the crook of his arm, and she relaxed even more in spite of her confusion. It felt so entirely natural to be with him this way that some of her fears were eased.

"I went straight on up to Charlie's after I left you," he went on, "and I stayed quite a while because, when I got there, Thad and Rowena were there, and I didn't want to talk in front of them."

He paused to brush away a strand of her hair that had fallen toward her eyes, and her throat tightened at the gentleness of his touch. She felt the sudden sting of tears trembling on the edges of her lids and looked away so that he wouldn't see. The worn gray brown boards of the porch floor blurred in front of her.

"Then I told him how much money would be involved and how it would make him a lot more comfortable for the rest of his life," he said. "I mentioned medical care and upkeep on his place and something to leave to Thad and Rowena."

"And?"

"And he said, 'No. No, thank ye, son. I know you're accustomed to takin' ever'thing ye can and makin' money from it. And I know ye've got my good at heart, too. But I never could sell ye my story.' Then he shifted his tobacco around in his jaw and . . ."

Vance pulled back so that he could see her face. "You know that tone of voice he uses when he's saying his last word on a subject?"

She nodded, smiling.

"Well, in that tone, he said, 'I jist wouldn't feel right makin' a profit on somethin' so dear to me as that.'"

As he finished recounting the experience Vance's eyes bored into hers, almost black with the intensity of his feelings. "Lane, those words pounded in my head all the time I was in New York on business. It's really true that to some people there are lots of things more important than money."

"I know," she answered, her mind flashing in quick succession from Charlie's loyalty to Alice's old love to Thad and Rowena's new one—and to the feelings that were flooding her heart at that very moment.

"Well, I want to learn about some of them. I told you that I've been looking for something besides more companies and more profits for a long time now."

"I know, Vance, and I hope you find it."

His hand closed around her arm, and when he spoke his voice was husky. "I think I already have."

She didn't dare look up at him. She didn't dare move. Instead she stared across the narrow valley, across the tops of the trees that concealed the merrymakers far below. "What is it?"

"Remember when you said that these Appalachian people have some qualities that ought to be preserved and shared with the rest of the country?"

"Yes, that was the lecture I gave you at The Woodfern."

He chuckled. "Well, I've taken it to heart at last, and I've made a decision about how to accomplish some of the sharing and preservation."

"You have?" Excitement thrilled in her voice. "How?"

"Tell you in a minute," he teased. He tilted her chin up so she could see his impish grin and bent to kiss her again, very quickly, tantalizingly. A thrill of wordless communication ran through her. Now he knew. He had learned for himself what she'd been trying to tell him.

She pushed him away playfully. "You tell me now," she ordered. "What are you going to do?"

"I'm changing Greenbriar completely."

"How? What do you mean? *What are you going to do?*"

"Hey," he said, laughing. "Wait. Listen to the plan. Greenbriar is no longer going to be just another amusement park like the other ones I own. Instead I'm going to make it a living experience of the past, sort of a re-creation of mountain life in the old days."

She sat up very straight, her pulse thudding with excitement. "You mean like Williamsburg?"

He nodded. "Something on that order, yes." His smile was broad and full of light. "What do you think?"

"I think it's the perfect idea!"

"So do I. Can't you just see it? We'll have all these log cabins and open-air workshops, and Charlie can come and cut notches in logs and talk about all the different kinds—"

"And Polly Clay can quilt," she interrupted breathlessly. "And Addie Keanan can set up her pots and dye yarn, and Andy can make brooms. . . ."

"Exactly. And Thad can bring his band and play hoedowns so we can all dance all day long."

"Oh, Vance! This is terrific. I can't wait! How long will it be before it's in operation?"

He chuckled. "That largely depends on you, I hope," he answered.

"On me?"

"I want you to manage it. I want you to oversee all the planning and the hiring and the other arrangements so that everything will be as authentic as possible."

He smiled at her, enjoying the succession of expressions racing across her face. His finger traced the curve of her cheek. "I'm offering you a job, Lane. Will you take it? Will you direct Greenbriar for me?"

Wide-eyed, she just stared at him, unable for a minute to take everything in. It would be wonderful. It would be the most fabulous job she could ever imagine having.

But she would be working with him; she'd be close to him, maybe as close as this every day. "So we can dance all day," he'd said. Could she do that? Could she cope with that if they had no commitment to each other?

She'd thought they were about to say good-bye. Now it seemed that they weren't. But how could she bear to be beside him every day, to look into his laughing brown eyes, to hear his voice, to touch his hand . . . how could she possibly bear it if he didn't belong to her forever?

He kept watching her face and, as if he'd read her thoughts he put one finger under her chin and turned her face to him. He was very close, and when he opened his mouth to speak, the warm sweetness of his breath brushed her mouth.

"Lane . . ."

Then his touch feathered down the side of her throat, setting every nerve in her body on fire, and his lips were against hers. They moved surely over her mouth, caressing it, loving it, trying to tell her something.

His tongue didn't ask this time. It demanded entrance to her mouth as if it belonged there. It explored every inch of it with a wild, pulsing abandon, with luxurious care, as if he had been away from her for too long. His big hand spanned the small of her back and pressed her to him.

His other hand went hungrily to cup her head, and his long fingers drove into her hair, parting it and tangling in it, taking possession of it and of all of her as he pressed her to him.

Panic mixed with the hot desire racing through her, and she turned her mouth away. "Vance . . ." she whispered.

He let her move only enough so that he could see her face. "Don't," he said, his voice very low and quietly commanding. "Don't talk and don't give me an answer to my question yet because I have another one to ask you."

She obeyed, staring into the dark lights that were in his eyes. He was so intense that every line of his face seemed to be carved from stone.

He became very still, and his words fell quietly into the lush afternoon. "Once you said, 'A passion like ours is too much for me to handle if it's just a temporary amusement for you.' Do you remember that?"

Wordlessly, she nodded.

"Lane, there's nothing temporary about it for me. I love you with my life and I want this passion we have to last forever."

Her heart stopped beating, and she thought it would never start up again. His loving words were twined around it, holding it still with wonder.

He moved closer so that once again their lips were only a breath apart. "Lane, will you marry me?" His beguiling smile was full of mischief. "You can take your time deciding about the job, but I have to have an answer to this question within the next ten seconds."

A breeze floated around the corner of the porch and ruffled his hair; it brought the chirpings of birds from farther up the mountain, and suddenly this day was the most beautiful one of her entire life.

The smile she gave him blazed with all the joy that was in her heart. She just had time to whisper, "Oh, yes, my love. Oh, yes!" before he cradled her face in the hollow of his hand and brought her lips to his to begin another kiss.

Silhouette Special Edition. Romances for the woman who expects a little more out of love.

If you enjoyed this book, and you're ready for more great romance

…get 4 romance novels FREE when you become a Silhouette Special Edition home subscriber.

Act now and we'll send you four exciting Silhouette Special Edition romance novels. They're our gift to introduce you to our convenient home subscription service. Every month, we'll send you six new passion-filled Special Edition books. Look them over for 15 days. If you keep them, pay just $11.70 for all six. Or return them at no charge.

We'll mail your books to you two full months *before they are available anywhere else.* Plus, with every shipment, you'll receive the Silhouette Books Newsletter absolutely free. *And with Silhouette Special Edition there are never any shipping or handling charges.*

Mail the coupon today to get your four free books—and more romance than you ever bargained for.

Silhouette Special Edition is a service mark and a registered trademark of Simon & Schuster, Inc.

MAIL COUPON TODAY

Silhouette Special Edition
120 Brighton Road, P.O. Box 5020, Clifton, N.J. 07015

☐ Yes, please send me FREE and without obligation, 4 exciting Silhouette Special Edition romance novels. Unless you hear from me after I receive my 4 FREE BOOKS, please send me 6 new books to preview each month. I understand that you will bill me just $1.95 each for a total of $11.70—with no additional shipping, handling or other charges. **There is no minimum number of books that I must buy, and I can cancel anytime I wish.** The first 4 books are mine to keep, even if I never take a single additional book.

☐ Mrs. ☐ Miss ☐ Ms. ☐ Mr.   BSS2R4

Name _____ (please print)

Address _____ Apt. No. _____

City _____ State _____ Zip _____

Signature (If under 18, parent or guardian must sign.)

This offer, limited to one per customer, expires August 31, 1984. Terms and prices subject to change. Your enrollment is subject to acceptance by Simon & Schuster Enterprises.

MORE ROMANCE FOR
A SPECIAL WAY TO RELAX
$1.95 each

2 ☐ Hastings	23 ☐ Charles	45 ☐ Charles	66 ☐ Mikels
3 ☐ Dixon	24 ☐ Dixon	46 ☐ Howard	67 ☐ Shaw
4 ☐ Vitek	25 ☐ Hardy	47 ☐ Stephens	68 ☐ Sinclair
5 ☐ Converse	26 ☐ Scott	48 ☐ Ferrell	69 ☐ Dalton
6 ☐ Douglass	27 ☐ Wisdom	49 ☐ Hastings	70 ☐ Clare
7 ☐ Stanford	28 ☐ Ripy	50 ☐ Browning	71 ☐ Skillern
8 ☐ Halston	29 ☐ Bergen	51 ☐ Trent	72 ☐ Belmont
9 ☐ Baxter	30 ☐ Stephens	52 ☐ Sinclair	73 ☐ Taylor
10 ☐ Thiels	31 ☐ Baxter	53 ☐ Thomas	74 ☐ Wisdom
11 ☐ Thornton	32 ☐ Douglass	54 ☐ Hohl	75 ☐ John
12 ☐ Sinclair	33 ☐ Palmer	55 ☐ Stanford	76 ☐ Ripy
13 ☐ Beckman	35 ☐ James	56 ☐ Wallace	77 ☐ Bergen
14 ☐ Keene	36 ☐ Dailey	57 ☐ Thornton	78 ☐ Gladstone
15 ☐ James	37 ☐ Stanford	58 ☐ Douglass	79 ☐ Hastings
16 ☐ Carr	38 ☐ John	59 ☐ Roberts	80 ☐ Douglass
17 ☐ John	39 ☐ Milan	60 ☐ Thorne	81 ☐ Thornton
18 ☐ Hamilton	40 ☐ Converse	61 ☐ Beckman	82 ☐ McKenna
19 ☐ Shaw	41 ☐ Halston	62 ☐ Bright	83 ☐ Major
20 ☐ Musgrave	42 ☐ Drummond	63 ☐ Wallace	84 ☐ Stephens
21 ☐ Hastings	43 ☐ Shaw	64 ☐ Converse	85 ☐ Beckman
22 ☐ Howard	44 ☐ Eden	65 ☐ Cates	86 ☐ Halston

Silhouette Special Edition

$2.25 each

87 ☐ Dixon	103 ☐ Taylor	119 ☐ Langan	135 ☐ Seger
88 ☐ Saxon	104 ☐ Wallace	120 ☐ Dixon	136 ☐ Scott
89 ☐ Meriwether	105 ☐ Sinclair	121 ☐ Shaw	137 ☐ Parker
90 ☐ Justin	106 ☐ John	122 ☐ Walker	138 ☐ Thornton
91 ☐ Stanford	107 ☐ Ross	123 ☐ Douglass	139 ☐ Halston
92 ☐ Hamilton	108 ☐ Stephens	124 ☐ Mikels	140 ☐ Sinclair
93 ☐ Lacey	109 ☐ Beckman	125 ☐ Cates	141 ☐ Saxon
94 ☐ Barrie	110 ☐ Browning	126 ☐ Wildman	142 ☐ Bergen
95 ☐ Doyle	111 ☐ Thorne	127 ☐ Taylor	143 ☐ Bright
96 ☐ Baxter	112 ☐ Belmont	128 ☐ Macomber	144 ☐ Meriwether
97 ☐ Shaw	113 ☐ Camp	129 ☐ Rowe	145 ☐ Wallace
98 ☐ Hurley	114 ☐ Ripy	130 ☐ Carr	146 ☐ Thornton
99 ☐ Dixon	115 ☐ Halston	131 ☐ Lee	147 ☐ Dalton
100 ☐ Roberts	116 ☐ Roberts	132 ☐ Dailey	148 ☐ Gordon
101 ☐ Bergen	117 ☐ Converse	133 ☐ Douglass	149 ☐ Claire
102 ☐ Wallace	118 ☐ Jackson	134 ☐ Ripy	150 ☐ Dailey

SILHOUETTE SPECIAL EDITION, Department SE/2
1230 Avenue of the Americas
New York, NY 10020

Please send me the books I have checked above. I am enclosing $_____
(please add 75¢ to cover postage and handling. NYS and NYC residents please
add appropriate sales tax). Send check or money order—no cash or C.O.D.'s
please. Allow six weeks for delivery.

NAME _____

ADDRESS _____

CITY _____ STATE/ZIP _____

Love, passion and adventure will be yours FREE for 15 days... with Tapestry™ historical romances!

"Long before women could read and write, tapestries were used to record events and stories . . . especially the exploits of courageous knights and their ladies."

And now there's a new kind of tapestry...

In the pages of Tapestry™ romance novels, you'll find love, intrigue, and historical touches that really make the stories come alive!

You'll meet brave Guyon d'Arcy, a Norman knight . . . handsome Comte Andre de Crillon, a Huguenot royalist . . . rugged Branch Taggart, a feuding American rancher . . . and more. And on each journey back in time, you'll experience tender romance and searing passion . . . and learn about the way people lived and loved in earlier times than ours.

We think you'll be so delighted with Tapestry romances, you won't want to miss a single one! We'd like to send you 2 books each month, as soon as they are published, through our Tapestry Home Subscription Service.℠ Look them over for 15 days, free. If not delighted, simply return them and owe nothing. But if you enjoy them as much as we think you will, pay the invoice enclosed. There's never any additional charge for this convenient service — we pay all postage and handling costs.

To receive your Tapestry historical romances, fill out the coupon below and mail it to us today. You're on your way to all the love, passion, and adventure of times gone by!

HISTORICAL *Tapestry* ROMANCES

Tapestry Home Subscription Service
120 Brighton Road, Box 5020, Clifton, NJ 07012

Yes, I'd like to receive 2 exciting Tapestry historical romances each month as soon as they are published. The books are mine to examine for 15 days, free. If not delighted, I can return them and owe nothing. There is never a charge for this convenient home delivery—no postage, handling, or any other hidden charges. If I decide to keep the books, I will pay the invoice enclosed.

I understand there is no minimum number of books I must buy, and that I can cancel this arrangement at any time.

Name

Address

City   State   Zip

Signature   (If under 18, parent or guardian must sign.)   BTS2P4

This offer expires August 31, 1984

Tapestry™ is a trademark of Simon & Schuster.

Watch for

NORA ROBERTS'

PROMISE ME TOMORROW

Coming in February

from

Pocket Books.

Available at your local bookstore

Silhouette Special Edition

Coming Next Month

A Love Song And You by Linda Shaw

By all rights Laura Remington and country and western star Dallas Jones should have been enemies. But nothing seemed to matter but the magnetic energy that charged the atmosphere when they were together.

Gentle Possession by Melodie Adams

Caleb Stone and Randi Warner had a contract: he needed a son and she needed to pay her father's debt. Randi fulfilled her part of the bargain, but how could she leave Caleb when through their child they found the promise of forever?

The Tangled Web by Tracy Sinclair

Trapped in a deception, Nicole never thought she'd find herself drawn to the man she'd schemed to deceive. But falling in love with Flint Lockridge could put her at his mercy—and completely destroy her plans.

A Ruling Passion by Doreen Owens Malek

Try as she might, journalist Megan Fielding couldn't keep her objectivity when she was around Mike Henley. He touched her as no man ever had, but could she do her job and keep Michael as well?

Softly At Sunset by Anne Lacey

Tragedy had touched Cade Thornton's family, and Jill had the task of healing his daughter's pain. Soon her tenderness extended to the father as well, and her job of healing was complicated by new feelings of love.

Tell Me No Lies by Brooke Hastings

Maggie got a kick out of masquerading as an eighteen year old student to get an audition with director Carson McDermitt. But the joke was on her, for how could her growing passion for him be indulged when he was fighting his feelings for the woman he thought of as a young girl?